CHAPTER

ONE

Tom Janos drummed his fingertips against each other as he endured the girl's babbling. He already knew where her story was headed when she told him where she had gone for dinner, but she never used ten words when she could use fifty. Tom had learned long ago that the best way to keep his people in line was to let them tell stories in their own ways. Even so, it took him every ounce of effort to refrain from throttling her. He nodded with concern, never taking his eyes off hers, as she continued prattling breathlessly.

"So I finished my chicken sandwich," Marissa Meyer said. "I didn't get a hamburger, because I don't eat meat, even though they've sold billions of them, so I guess they must, like, be okay. The chicken sandwich wasn't as good — I mean, it *probably* wasn't as good — as the ones they sell at the place across the street, but *that* place has the most *awful* policies about reproductive health care for their employees, and how could I in good conscience eat food that, like, *oppresses women*, you know?"

"Of course," said Tom, with beatific patience.

"Well," she continued, "I stepped out and was looking right at that other place, and thinking about those poor

women who work for them and can't get abortions or even *the pill*, when two buses started unloading. And I was just *offended* that they were going to make so much money from that crowd, when there was a *perfectly* good hamburger place across the street that served chicken sandwiches and even hired *black* people. And I wouldn't have gone over there at *all*, except I saw…"

Here she started to chew on her fingernail nervously. Tom pursed his lips. "Marissa," he said. "Go on. What disturbed you so?"

The girl, Marissa Meyer, looked up at the serene face of the leader of the protest group — the man who had offered her a place in line, a sign to hold, and twenty-five dollars a day plus meals and lodging, so she and others could demand justice — 'justice' coming in the form of removing a one-hundred-year-old statue of a Confederate soldier.

Tom Janos's dark hair was slicked to one side, and his blue eyes looked not so much at her as through her. But he was a good man, she knew. Such a good man, in fact, that she couldn't make sense of what she had seen.

"What did you see?" Tom asked.

"I saw the buses unloading," she said meekly. "And those people on the bus, they were — they had *shirts*, and those awful red hats that said 'Make Patriotism Fashionable Again.' Some of them even had little *flags* with them — and not rainbow or Mexican ones, but actual *American* flags! Well, I knew right away they must have come here to cause trouble."

"They probably did," Tom said.

"That's why I couldn't figure out why you were with them," she said.

Tom Janos arched an eyebrow. "You must be mistaken," he said. "I've been here all evening, meeting with other marchers, making sure they know when things happen, what they can say and do, and how to avoid getting arrested. It must have been someone who looked like me. You were across the street, after all."

"I was," she said. "But then I wasn't. I mean, I went over because I knew that it couldn't be you — I mean, it *couldn't* — but I had to be sure. And I stayed quiet because I didn't want to let any of them know I was here to have that *awful* monument to racism removed, because there were just so *many* of them."

"You went over to them," Tom repeated, trying to keep Marissa from veering off-topic again. He stood and walked to the window of his room, and looked out over the parking lot of the hotel. The city of Little Rock was clearly visible to the west, not so much as a skyline but as a cluster.

The Man Upstairs had been right. These southern cities were powder kegs, ready and waiting to be lit. That was what made protests in the South different from protests in New England or the Pacific Northwest — the people of Dixie actually cared about their flags, statues, and way of life.

"Yes sir, I did," she said.

"And then what?"

"Well, I went up to the man that looked like you, and he turned around, and then I was sure it was you." Marissa wrinkled her nose up in confusion, widening her nostril in the process so that the back side of her nose piercing was visible. "So I said, 'Excuse me, Mister Janos?' And he looked at me and — and he said, 'Can I help you, darlin'?' He said it *just like*

that, like he was from Texas or something."

"He did, did he?" Tom said. "Well, that's very strange."

"Do you think they know we're here?" Marissa said. "Maybe they know you hired us, and they went out and got a lookalike to confuse people?"

Tom Janos spun around, displaying a theatrical shocked expression. "Goodness, do you think they might be that clever?" he asked, his eyes wide with surprise.

"Maybe!", she exclaimed, caught up in the energy of his performance. "Do you think we should let everybody know, just to be careful?"

"Oh, definitely not," Tom said. He walked over and squatted down in front of her. "You haven't told anyone else so far, have you?" His eyes bored into hers, so pale and clear blue.

"No," Marissa said. "I ran straight back here to the hotel to tell you. And here you were, so I guess it really couldn't have been you."

"That's right, Marissa," Tom said. "It wasn't me. Now, listen carefully. Don't tell anybody. You're probably right about their plans. But they don't know we know, do they?" He winked. "If we keep this secret, keep it from getting out, we can turn it back on them, throw them into disarray, right?"

Marissa's eyes widened. "Oh, that's brilliant, Mister Janos! They could think *you* were *their* lookalike! You could tell them to turn around and go the other way, or to let us up in front, or even send them all back home! You are so, *so* smart!"

"Well, I get by," he said modestly. He took her by the hand and stood her up. "Now, Marissa, it's important we keep this a secret, you understand? I want you to go straight to your room

---

4

for the night. Talk to nobody. In the morning, go with everyone to the park as though none of this happened."

"Okay, but can't I help with —"

"Shh." He put his finger to her lips. "You don't have to do anything but focus on holding signs and chanting lines," he said. "Leave everything else to me."

Marissa Meyer flushed, a pinkness spreading across her cheeks that almost matched that of the homemade crocheted cap she wore. She paused in the expectation of something more. But Tom went briskly to the door and held it open. Obediently, she left and went straight to her room without speaking to another soul.

When she was out of sight, Tom Janos put out the 'Do Not Disturb' sign and turned the deadbolt. Then he took a sticky note with the logo of the hotel chain from the desk and placed it over the door's peephole before taking out his cell phone and tapping in a number.

After a few rings, the screen lit up to a streaming video, and a face identical to that of Tom Janos.

"What's up, little brother," the face said.

Tom smirked. "'Little' by four minutes, Bob," he said. "And only because you pushed me out of the way."

"Still counts."

Tom's face quickly turned serious. "We have a small problem." He recounted the story Marissa Meyer had told him in a matter of moments.

"They do have the best chicken sandwiches," Bob Janos said when he was done.

"I know," Tom said. "Next time, you get *this* group. I had to eat kale salad with pine nuts."

"I can send you over a spicy chicken sandwich," Bob offered.

Tom considered the offer for a brief moment. "Maybe later," he said. "What should we do about the girl?"

"I remember her," said Bob. "Figured she wanted to sleep with me, but got too intimidated."

"Pretty sure she wants to sleep with me," Tom said.

"Then let her," Bob replied. "But better do it quick. I say we remove her, just to be safe. If you want, I've got a few 'true believers' on this side who are just itching to put a Fascist Fighter in a hole in the ground. Of course, we should get clearance on that first."

Tom nodded. "My thoughts exactly. I'll call you back."

He disconnected the call and dialed in another number from memory. This one answered on the first ring. There was no video.

Tom related the story again, even more tersely than he had with his brother. "What would you like us to do, sir?" he asked when finished.

The electronically-masked voice gave a two-word response, then disconnected.

Immediately, Tom called Bob again. "We have clearance," he said. He unfolded his map of the park where the protests were planned. On the other end, Bob was doing the same. "Here's where she'll be."

• • •

Roger Whitman was hard core. If you did not believe him, he would show you his fists. He had had the words tattooed onto his hands, one letter per knuckle. Unfortunately, he had done it himself, and so what read HARD CORE to him when

he looked at his fists read CORE HARD to anyone else who saw them.

Roger Whitman believed in America — the *real* America he was trying to take back; the *white* America, before all the Blacks and Mexicans came over to take all their benefits and jobs; the *good* America where men worked, women made babies, and pansies and fairies were taken on rides from which they did not come back. He believed that even today, even after his wife got infected with feminist ideas, like that he drank too much and hit her too many times, and took it into her head to run off with the kids — *his* kids.

These thoughts ran through his mind as he looked out over the dashboard at the crowd of hippy-dippy faggots trying to erase the history of his America. Most of these self-styled Fascist Fighters were too chickenshit to even show their faces, hiding behind bandanas and plastic Halloween masks. But Roger was not being paid to look at them, so he forced himself to look past them, toward the grove of trees just beyond the curb. Just as he had been told, there was the girl. She was holding up the big pink sign with white letters — *white* letters, of all the nerve! — proclaiming her message: MAKE AN IMPACT ON RACISM.

Making an impact is exactly what Roger had in mind, as he stomped on the gas pedal and shifted the SUV into drive.

Roger knew the plan. Spot the girl. Hit the girl. Hit the tree behind the girl. Get cushioned by the airbags. Get arrested. Plead self-defense.

It was a perfect plan.

And it *was* a perfect plan. Roger just did not know all of it. The crowd scattered as he accelerated into it. Some of them

screamed, some of them smacked his hood as he plowed through, but they all got out of the way. Roger laughed as they ran, the way cockroaches skittered away when a light was turned on.

Yards ahead, Marissa Meyer held her sign just the way she had been told, surrounded by others who were peacefully throwing glass bottles at the police and counter-protesters. She stared with disbelief at the approaching vehicle. Surely someone was going to stop it, right? It could not be allowed to just drive over the curb…and onto the grass…and into…

…her.

And then the tree.

Roger carried out the plan to the letter, playing his part perfectly — even the part he did not know about, which involved flying through the windshield.

As his face smashed through the glass, he briefly wondered why the airbags had not gone off the way Bob Janos promised they would. That was supposed to be the plan, after all.

As Roger Whitman lay bleeding out, yards away a crowd quickly formed around Marissa Meyer. Her mouth gaped open, as the grill of the SUV squashed her midsection against the thick trunk of the tree behind her. Her blood pooled at the roots and tires.

Across the street, Bob Janos grimly observed the chaos. The plan — his plan — had worked just as expected.

Now there was nobody alive who would learn Marissa Meyer's secret, and nobody alive to learn why Roger Whitman was instructed to mow her down.

CHAPTER TWO

HIS NAME WAS REMO, AND HE WAS crossing the Oregon border into Mexico. The streets of Portland were still visible through the bars of the wrought iron fence surrounding the Mexican consulate, an impenetrable wall demarcating the land on one side as Mexican sovereign territory, separate and segregated from the United States.

The irony was not lost on him.

Dressed in a tight-fitting black t-shirt and black chinos, Remo Williams was a shadow flitting rapidly up the iron bars, a shadow that quickly flipped over the spiked top, dropped noiselessly on the opposite side, and was gone. The distance from the fence to the main structure was easily covered in a few paces, and the stucco exterior was almost insultingly easy to grip as Remo pressed his body against the wall and began scaling his way upward, sometimes sideways, sometimes diagonally, until he reached the window he was looking for.

With his right hand gripping the wall, he spread the fingers of his left hand and placed it against the glass. His fingertips slightly curved, he swiveled his wrist back and forth, his nails leaving white trails on the glass like ice skates on a frozen pond until he had carved a perfect circle in the glass. When he

was satisfied with the results, he gently tapped the upper portion of the circle. As the glass tumbled inward, his hand darted into the freshly made hole and caught the falling circle between his thumb and index finger, drawing it back out the window and slipping it into his pocket. Then, reaching once more into the window, he slowly moved his open palm in an arc, feeling for the tingle of the electronic alarm system. Finding the wire he sought, he traced it with his fingertip until he found where the magnetic receiver was mounted.

With a quick snap, he cracked both sides of the magnetic sensor from the window, keeping the two halves together as he set them quietly on the sill. The alarm now disabled, he silently unlocked the window, pushed it up, and slid inside as softly as a breeze.

Hector Suarez snored lightly, his arm draped across the bare back of a dark-haired woman sleeping beside him. Remo placed his hand against the side of her neck and gently pressed, ensuring her sleep would be uninterrupted for a few more hours. Then he patted Hector's cheek.

"Wakey, wakey, eggs and bakey."

Hector woke with a start. The face looking down at him was like Death. The skin was pulled tight against the cheekbones; the eyes were sunk deep beneath the brow. His first instinct was to call for a guard, but the man's hand flashed out, and the tips of his fingers brushed across Hector's throat. Hector grabbed his neck with both hands, then pulled them away to inspect his palms for blood. There was none — yet he could not even muster a whisper.

"No need to get excited, Hector," Remo said. "I'm just here to praise you on your business acumen and philanthropy."

Hector mouthed, "*¿Qué?*" but no sound came out.

Remo held up his hand. "You don't have to thank me," he said. "I'm honored, truly. It's quite the thing you've done, saving all those people."

Hector tried to sit up, but he was thrust forcefully back onto his mattress. The nubile girl next to him did not stir.

"I must insist on you letting me sing your praises just a little more," Remo said pleasantly. "I mean, it's not every day one meets someone who's changed as many lives as you have." He sat on the edge of the bed. "I imagine all those girls can't speak highly enough of you."

Hector tried to push himself back up, to fight, or to run. But his arms would not cooperate. He tried thrusting his torso forward into a sitting position, only to be quickly and firmly pushed back down with a palm to the forehead.

"As I was saying," Remo continued. "I applaud your altruism. I mean, you had diplomatic immunity and clear passage to Mexico. Surely there was a way you could use that to help somebody, right? And, by golly, you found the way. All those regular trips with no border crossing checks? That's just screaming for things to be brought across the border with you, isn't it?" Remo grabbed Hector's scalp and forced his head forward and backward in a nod. "Say, 'Yes, it is.'"

Hector moved his lips, but no sound came out.

"Now, a lot of guys in your position, they'd bring in drugs or guns," Remo said. "I mean, that's easy money, right? But that's not very charitable, is it? No, you're a better man than

that. You've seen first-hand the crappy conditions those people have to live in. And you could get them out of that so easily."

Remo clapped his hands together, softly and silently. "I applaud you, sir. Well done." He reached over and put two fingers to the side of Hector's larynx, and pressed until it popped.

Hector coughed. "*¿Gracias?*" he wheezed.

"You deserve it," Remo said warmly. "All those girls, so eager to have an opportunity. And it didn't hurt that they were so pretty, did it?" he winked.

"Are you…" Hector rasped. He swallowed, trying to ease the soreness in his throat. "Are you wanting in? Wanting a special order?"

"Oh, no," Remo said. "I've already got a job. And I'm not really in the market for what you're selling. That is what you're doing with the girls, right? Selling them? Sure, you bring them to America, just like you promised them. But then you exchange them for cash to someone who takes them right back out, smooth as silk."

Hector was confused. The man was obviously a threat, but he was talking about what a good job Hector was doing. And he did not want to muscle in on Hector's business, which Hector would have allowed until he could have the man killed. The man did not even want a girl, which Hector could not believe.

"A boy?" Hector asked. "I can get you a boy. I can get you lots of boys. Good price, too."

Remo smiled grimly and shook his head. "You don't

understand, Hector. You had a great business model, taking desperate ladies out of little shithole countries and finding them homes in slightly less shithole countries. Everybody wins, and nobody complains. See, that's my business. I'm the Complaint Department, and nobody ever said a word to me. Until you got greedy."

"No," Hector croaked. "No, never. My prices are always fair!"

"Sure, sure," Remo said. "I mean, if anyone ever had a fair price on a human life, it was you. But somewhere along the way, you noticed your supply chain was only profitable in one direction. You were coming back fully packed, but going down with an empty load. That's a wasted trip. Money on the table, right? So being an enterprising entrepreneur, you figured you'd work the system both directions, and start taking American girls south of the border. The embassy has lots of parties, right? You invite stupid young kids off the street, pretty girls looking to be actresses and models, and offer them a chance to see Margaritaville up close and personal. Who would turn that down?"

Remo's gaze turned serious. "And once down there," he said, "you sell them to off to your warlords, drug cartel honchos, and other run-of-the-mill bad hombres." He wagged his finger at Hector. "Hence the complaints." He stood. "My department."

"Complaints?" Hector rasped. "I have had no complaints, *señor*."

"No, you wouldn't have," Remo said, pacing along the side of the bed. "You see, I work for a sort of 'anonymous

consumer affairs' organization. They're like the Better Business Bureau, only better, and a lot stricter. And they really don't like it when someone starts carting our citizens away to other countries against their will. That's when they send in someone like me. Well, just me, actually."

Remo spoke the truth. The agency he worked for, CURE, consisted of only two people — himself, and the man who gave him his missions. It had been that way ever since the day Remo had found his police career cut short, having been framed for the murder of a drug dealer and summarily executed. But the execution was a sham, orchestrated by CURE so that Remo could become a man who did not exist. Trained by the ancient Master of Sinanju, Chiun, Remo Williams was now the deadliest man alive, and a practitioner of the most revered form of public service in all history: assassination.

"I can't move my arms."

"Oh. Right," said Remo. "That's not really fair, is it? Here, let me." Remo placed his palms on both shoulders and shifted them upward, releasing the nerve clusters he had pinched off earlier. Hector grunted as a dull pain flowed down both arms, and he curled his fingers to test his mobility.

"There you go," Remo said. "Good as new." He patted Hector on the chest twice.

"You'll never...never..." Hector sat up, possibly with the intention of confronting this *diablo misterioso*, when his chest suddenly felt like a bowling ball had been dropped inside it. "*¿Qué...?*"

"All part of the service," Remo said. "It's hard to be an

assassin who doesn't exist if you leave a trail of obvious bodies behind you. Believe me, a messy job just means a lot of cleanup, and I hate cleaning up."

Hector coughed, then gasped for air as he beat his fist against his sternum. "*Por favor*," he pleaded.

"See, I was never here," Remo continued. "And you simply made the mistake of overestimating your ability to keep up with this lovely young thing you brought to your bed tonight." He picked up the phone from the nightstand beside Hector's bed. "And in your panic, you fumbled with the numbers on your phone but couldn't make your fingers work, so you used it the best way you could to summon help." Remo sent the phone hurtling toward the window he had come in, shattering it and obliterating the neat circular hole he had cut into it.

Remo looked curiously at the window as if he had expected more. "Oh, right," he said. He slapped his forehead in a show of forgetfulness. "How silly of me. The alarm's off."

As Hector's last breath rattled in his chest, he saw the thin man in black pick up the magnetic trigger for the window alarm and pulled the two pieces apart, breaking the circuit and setting off the jangling alarm system.

Within moments, a trio of guards burst through Hector's bedroom door, finding the diplomatic envoy lifeless and alone save for the deeply-tanned, naked teenager who slept peacefully through the chaos.

There was no indication anyone else had ever been in the room.

CHAPTER THREE

THE SPARTAN OFFICES OF Dr. Harold W. Smith had, for several of the past years, been a quiet place where Smith could focus on his work. Despite having the official title as Senior Administrator of Folcroft Sanitarium, Smith's actual work involved overseeing a completely different operation, for which the little mental health retreat in Rye, New York was simply a convenient cover.

Harold Smith was one half of a secret government agency known only to three people: himself, Remo Williams, and the President of the United States. It had been his duty as the Director of CURE to monitor current events, isolate patterns of corruption, and identify the root causes of actions that threatened the country. If these root causes could be handled by conventional means, the evidence would find its way through channels to appropriate law enforcement.

At those times when conventional means could not be called upon, however — when the Constitution itself prevented the country from acting in its own best defense — Smith had the license to send in unconventional means.

Those means were Remo Williams.

Smith had served under several presidents in this capacity,

ever since his appointment decades ago by a President with the foresight to see the country needed an entity like CURE. And while every President since had known of its existence, and of its necessity, the only power any president had over CURE was the authority to disband the organization; they could not direct CURE to carry out specific assignments.

This latest President had needed a bit more reminding than most, and answering the direct line to the Oval Office that had remained almost entirely disused for the better part of a decade had now become a part of his daily routine.

Smith remotely monitored the daily White House intelligence briefing, as he always did. Then, when it had concluded, he turned toward the black rotary phone and waited. Within thirty seconds, it rang.

"Yes, Mister President?" Smith answered with practiced patience.

"Smith, can't your guy do something about this immigration nightmare?"

Harold Smith did not sigh audibly. "I'm afraid not, sir," he replied calmly.

"But there's a damned invasion!"

"You have the Department of Homeland Security for that, sir."

The President sighed dramatically. "Yeah, well, every time I try that, some state files a lawsuit. Hey, what about this thing in Little Rock? The press is after my blood since that girl got run over."

Harold Smith looked at the monitor of the CURE

computer, countersunk beneath the glass overlay of his wooden desk and canted at such an angle as to be visible only to him. The CURE computer monitored events worldwide, comparing the minutest similarities in its tireless effort to examine patterns and raise alerts if something were found to be of interest to Smith. Indeed, the Little Rock event was ranking highly on the 3D wireframe model of potential problems CURE might need to solve.

Smith clicked on the item and watched as it expanded and unfolded its details into columns on the monitor. "Little Rock is something we are already aware of," Smith said. "And we are going to look into it."

"Can I tweet that?"

"I would recommend against it," Smith replied respectfully. Since the inauguration, the Smith had implemented new protocols and procedures to intercept the President's social media communications to ensure nothing remotely related to CURE would slip out, either by eliminating the communication altogether or scrambling key words into nonsense.

"Damn it, Smith, the country is forming into mobs," the President said. "I have to tell people something or it's going to look like we've lost control."

Smith entered more commands into the computer. The President was right: people *were* forming into mobs — mobs that confronted each other with increasing regularity. "Mr. President," Smith replied, "it is my experience that anything you say about the situation would only be used as an excuse

for more violence. If you say anything, offer condolences. Ask for people to find common ground."

"You think I haven't tried?" The President said. "Believe me, I've tried! I denounce the violence; they say I don't denounce it enough. I denounce it harder; they say I shouldn't blame both sides. I tell you, I can't win with these people. They're the only ones I can't win with. Everywhere else, I win. I win big. But not with these people."

As Smith listened, the pattern laid out by the CURE computer analysis algorithm was unmistakable. The screen began to populate with a multiple-column fact table of corresponding names and dollar values. Using next-generation facial recognition technology that would not be on the market for another decade, the CURE computer was able to identify a number of so-called "Fascist Fighters" by their eyes, using images pulled from social media coverage of their last three protests, including the one in Little Rock that had turned deadly. Each of the "Fascist Fighters" had received direct deposits three days prior to each event for $560.00.

Smith's naturally sour expression became more so. These were decidedly not the signs of a spontaneous, grassroots movement.

"We've tried that," the President said. "Look, I need something from your agency that can fix this. Do you need a bigger budget? I can get you a budget. Believe me, I can get you a big, beautiful budget. I can get you a budget like you've never seen."

"CURE's budget is well in hand, Mr. President, thank

you," Smith replied hurriedly, thankful Chiun was not present at the time. The ancient Master of Sinanju would prickle at Smith refusing more funding that could go to his home village in North Korea. "And I cannot tell you more, other than that we are concerned about the Little Rock matter, and will be investigating it thoroughly."

"You're going to send in your special guy, aren't you?"

"I'm afraid I've said all that I can without endangering your plausible deniability, Mr. President," Smith said. "I will be in touch."

Smith hung up one phone, opened a drawer in his desk to reveal another. This one was a digitally scrambled line that went directly to CURE's enforcement arm, Remo Williams.

"What now?" Remo answered.

"Is the tollway closed in both directions?" Smith asked flatly.

"It's a scrambled line, Smitty," Remo said. "I don't need *two* fortune cookie writers in my life."

"National security is no joke, Remo," Smith said.

"Fine, fine," Remo said. "Traffic is at a standstill in the southbound lanes," he added, repeating the memorized code phrase to indicate the successful termination of the ambassador.

"Understood," Smith said. His fingers entered a few quick commands at his keyboard. "There are tickets waiting for you at Sacramento International. I need you back at Folcroft as quickly as possible."

"Business is booming," Remo said.

Smith frowned at the phone, noting the almost exuberant tone of Remo's response. "Isn't this where you usually complain about having no downtime between missions?"

"What are you talking about, Smitty?" Remo said. "I'm itching and raring to go. Let's kill a commie for mommy."

"I'd like to speak with Master Chiun, please."

"Sure thing," Remo said. "I'll go pack."

Smith heard Remo call out for Chiun, getting a hushed string of Korean in return. A few moments later, "Greetings to you, oh gracious Emperor Smith, whose brilliance eclipses the sun itself." Chiun had, since his first meeting with Harold Smith, convinced himself that Smith was the shadow-emperor of the United States, in order to reconcile the traditions of Sinanju working exclusively for royalty. "How may the humble House of Sinanju be of service to his excellency?"

Smith got right to the point. "What's wrong with Remo?" he asked curtly.

"Many things," Chiun replied. "All of them shameful, but I can only do so much with him. Alas, it would be quicker should I list those things which are not wrong with my son. He is stubborn. He still strikes with his elbow bent. He undeniably lazy and tends toward being messy."

"Actually, his attitude is uncharacteristically positive," Smith said. "It's unlike him to be so eager for an assignment."

"It is natural for one to find satisfaction in one's chosen profession," Chiun said. "Even when it is performed with such mediocrity as my son is determined to employ."

In the background, Smith could hear Remo whistling as he packed his bags. He decided to try a different approach. "Master Chiun, from your privileged vantage point, have you observed Remo's behavior to be outside the norm?"

"Always has it been thus," Chiun said. "I cannot apologize enough for the ignominy my mercurial son has brought upon the House of Sinanju. I do my best to obfuscate his shortcomings in the sacred scrolls, but I fear that much more and I shall find myself engaging in outright prevarication."

"So, Remo is fine?" Smith asked.

Chiun huffed. "Never would I say that," he said. "Rather, I shall say that Remo is adequate, and I shall continue to watch over him closely."

Smith nodded to himself. "I appreciate that, Master Chiun," he said. "We will talk further upon your arrival at Folcroft."

• • •

Across the continent, looked at the screen of the phone until it reflected that the call had been terminated, then spared a sidelong glance at Remo.

"Zippa-dee doo-dah, Zippa-dee-yay," Remo hummed as he zipped up his travel case.

Chiun knew that Smith was correct, and there was something wrong with Remo. He knew precisely what it was, and from where it originated.

He would have to watch his son more closely than ever.

• • •

"I'm telling you, Chiun, I don't need any more

meditation," Remo said, bursting into the office of Harold Smith. The bickering upon entry was oddly reassuring for Smith. This was normal behavior, a status quo that meant all was right with the world.

"You can never meditate too much," Chiun said. "Can you breathe too much? Can you think too much?"

"You want to know what I think?" Remo asked.

"I would be satisfied to know *that* you think," Chiun said. "The *what* of it is beneath my concern."

Smith cleared his throat, the simple action getting the attention of both men.

"If we could get right to this?" Smith asked, archly.

"Sounds serious," Remo said, taking a seat opposite Smith's desk.

"It is always serious," Smith said without humor.

"Eh, not really," Remo replied. "Some of the things we deal with are pretty ridiculous."

"Two people are dead and more are likely," Smith deadpanned. "Is that serious enough for you?"

Remo shrugged. "We've seen worse. What's so special about this case?"

Smith summarily briefed Remo on the Little Rock riot that had resulted in the death of Marissa Meyer and, simultaneously, her assailant.

"So which people died?" Remo asked.

Smith blinked. "Did you hear anything I just said?"

"Yeah, yeah," Remo said. "One so-called Fascist Fighter, one neo-Nazi. So far, no *people*."

"Perhaps you haven't noticed while you've been traipsing about the country first class, but this nation has become a powder keg, and these two people may have lit the fuse," Smith said tersely. "A lot more deaths may be coming."

Remo's expression turned sober. "What do you want us to do about it?" he asked. "Go give everyone a good talking-to? Convince them to calm down and play nice?"

Chiun shook his head sadly. "This will not happen until Americans are at least as advanced as the Bonobo apes."

"Enough with the apes, already," Remo said, rolling his eyes. "You see one National Geographic special and suddenly you're Jane Goodall."

"They have no war," Chiun said. "They resolve conflicts peacefully."

"They throw their poop at you," said Remo.

"At least that much Americans have managed to emulate," the Master of Sinanju replied serenely. "There is far to go before the whites evolve further."

"In this instance, Master Chiun has a point."

Remo turned to Smith with a double take. "Excuse me?" he said.

"The behavior of the American public has devolved into increasingly-polarized camps," Smith said. "The last election only galvanized these feelings. But on their own, they're merely chaos. Chaos eventually dissipates — unless someone finds a way to impose order on it."

"So, you want us to find a way to impose order on chaos?" Remo asked.

"No," Smith replied. "I am saying that someone is already in the process of weaponizing national discontent." Smith passed Remo a printout of names, dates, and figures. "This is a list of identified protesters who marched with the Fascist Fighters in Little Rock. A search of their financial records found a disproportionate number of them received payments of similar amounts via direct deposits, from various political action committees and private charitable organizations."

"Someone's paying for malcontents," Remo nodded. "Do you have any idea who's the bankroll?"

Smith adjusted his glasses, and steepled his fingers. "Not yet, but I'm working on it," he said. "The situation is more complex than a matter of paid protesters."

"Paying the rabble to hold the opinion one wishes them to hold is tradition," Chiun said. "I am surprised Americans are so loath to embrace it. Nero himself paid audience members to applaud his singing, so that others would believe it must have some merit."

"Did it work?" Remo asked.

Chiun shrugged. "The people began to say he sang beautifully, though, of course, he did not. Truth is not decided by popular opinion. But Nero was a politician above all, and never are they interested in the truth when they consult the voice of the people." He turned to Remo. "Perhaps you should consider paying people to applaud your clumsy execution of Sinanju? It would not change the truth, but at least someone would tell you how good you are."

"Nero paid people to express one opinion," Smith

interjected before Remo could respond to Chiun's provocations. "That is not the case here." He gave Remo another printout, similar to the first. "These people were involved with the counter-protest. Their accounts showed the same activity as the Fascist Fighters."

Remo let out a low whistle. "Someone's playing both sides of the game," he said.

Smith pursed his lips, his expression dripping with more sourness than usual. "With that level of control, and public opinion already a bubbling cauldron of discontent..."

"Someone could start another civil war," Remo said, finishing Smith's thought.

"Exactly my concern," Smith nodded. "CURE needs you to infiltrate the paid protesters, follow the chain of command, and discover who is pulling the strings."

"Great," Remo said with enthusiasm. "Which set of Nazis do you want me to get in with?"

Chiun sniffed. "You are already too many decades late to find Nazis. All that remain are a few pale imitators who still delude themselves into thinking they are superior because they lack melanin in their skin."

"You're going to Billings, Montana," Smith said curtly. "An online advertisement has put out a call for paid protesters to audition there. Your credentials are waiting at the airport." Smith took the lists back from Remo.

"Your plane leaves in ninety minutes."

CHAPTER FOUR

THE CLICK OF Cheryl Sparks' heels echoed as she made her way down the marble hallway. The walls were lined with ornate busts and colorful tapestries, a genealogy in art of a proud family line.

It was not her family, of course. Her family lineage could be traced on the front page of the old family Bible that her grandmother kept, and none of the Sparks line had ever left Indiana since settling there — until Cheryl had a chance encounter with the powerful figure she now preparing to meet again.

Cheryl Sparks had made one impassioned plea on the Internet, one time, about how a tragic school shooting would never have occurred if only no one was allowed to have had guns in the first place. It was basic sense, she said.

Her approach to solving all problems involved this basic sense that no one else she knew seemed to possess. When opining on a horrible automobile accident, Cheryl had fought terribly to get people to realize that such loss of life could be avoided forever if people would simply stop driving cars. She made the argument all the time with the other moms in her car pool.

The night after the horrible school shooting, while the Internet was still buzzing with debates on whose fault it was, how easy guns were to get, and how we should not politicize the tragedy, Cheryl got an email from a name she vaguely recognized, asking for her thoughts on the scourge of gun violence.

She knew she had heard the man's name on the news before, and thought perhaps he was a reporter with one of the networks. But she soon learned that Hutch Pummel was a figure far more important to the dissemination of mass media than any mere talking head.

And now here she was, the head of the Heroines Against Guns movement, and thus an increasingly important media figure in her own right. The movement had rebranded itself, transitioning away from #WeaponWisdom to capitalize on a hit movie that promoted strong female values, and which featured a woman who could deflect bullets with the slave bracelets she wore on her wrists. Cheryl had decided to begin wearing such bracelets herself, to symbolically deflect all the bullets in the country. Her lower forearms had chafed into blisters, and a greenish tinge showed along the edges of the cheap metallic cuffs, but she refused to give them up.

A little discomfort and early-stage gangrene (which she was almost certain was the shade of coloration the bracelets produced, and why her doctor was so concerned about color she could not begin to imagine) was a small sacrifice to show solidarity with her fellow HAGs.

The hallway turned left, then quickly terminated at a large

set of oaken doors. The entrance would have looked more at home in a medieval castle than in a secluded Colorado mansion.

The past few years had nearly convinced her that if America had a secret king, Hutch Pummel would definitely be that man. A billionaire descendant of railroad barons, the Pummel family had built its money by controlling the distribution of all goods throughout the country, earning fractions of cents of profit every time goods were transported from one place to another. It was the slimmest of profit margins, but given the vast scale of Pummel's operations, it generated immeasurable wealth.

If ninety-five percent of the nation's wealth was controlled by five percent of the people, Hutch Pummel controlled ninety-five percent of that. With his financing, influence, and canny manipulation of the media, he had taken Cheryl's "basic sense" idea, and turned it into a real movement for change.

"Sorry I'm late," Cheryl announced as she pushed her way through the giant doors.

"Not at all, my dear," a hearty voice responded.

At the end of an epically long hardwood table, polished to a mirror shine, sat Hutch Pummel. His round, jovial face was mapped with laugh lines; his white hair, neatly combed to one side, was tipped with gray. "We wouldn't think of starting without you."

Other faces lining the sides of the table turned to look at her, their expressions showing their annoyance at having had to wait.

Cheryl did not care about them. They did not have to suffer the way she suffered, did not care as passionately as she did. She adjusted the metal bands on her forearms and took a seat in one of the high-backed chairs.

"I trust everyone is well," Pummel said in his usual avuncular way. "I've heard many good things, but I confess I don't hear everything. Does anyone have anything to share?"

Nobody took the initiative to speak.

"How about ladies first," Hutch offered with a smile. Contessa Shilling bristled at the sexist overtones of the old-fashioned offer, but quickly jumped up before Cheryl could.

"Our organization continues to march to promote feminine values," she said hoarsely. She jutted her chin forward proudly. "The vagina is fashionable once again."

"Quite literally fashionable," smirked Kirk Ehrlichman, a former sportscaster who had leveraged his name recognition to move into the realm of political commentary. "Those pink hats are quite something."

"It's all for equality," Shilling said. "There were already plenty of dickheads out there. Now we've struck a balance. Besides, it makes great optics on cable news — especially when we can get our male compatriots to dress up in labia jumpsuits. They get on camera every time."

She grinned conspiratorially. "All men are finally created equal, and it's made them women."

Those seated around the table politely clapped at Contessa's climactic statement.

"And how do you plan to progress from there?" Hutch

asked warmly. It was important that he keep them all thinking about next steps, particularly when those next steps would further his own interests.

Contessa thrust out her chin proudly. "We're going to protest the cable news networks!"

Hutch raised an eyebrow. "The platforms which have been carrying your message?" he asked. "Do you think that's wise?"

She shrugged. "What choice do we have?" she asked. "They allowed one of their guests to get away with saying 'boobs' on the airwaves. How demeaning! That phrase single-handedly set the woman's movement back a hundred years! Worse, it's left Americans with the impression that men can say whatever they want. One so-called 'alpha male,' with a national platform, might light a spark in the 'beta males' we've worked so hard to cultivate."

Hutch Pummel clucked with amusement. "Oh, I hardly think someone's puerile reference to female breasts is going to take away the woman's right to vote," he said. "But I do think you present an interesting case. You'd be able to pull eyeballs from various competing networks quite easily, I should imagine. They would love the opportunity to put their competition in a bad light. Get me a full proposal, and I'll approve the funding."

Hutch Pummel saw no reason to tell Contessa the guest had been booked with his approval, and passed through one of his subordinates, who had scripted both the question and the response — without letting either the interviewer or interviewee know they were being manipulated into a semantic

trap.

"Cheryl, how about you? Anything to add after your little…display in Dallas?"

Cheryl Sparks cleared her throat. "Our 'Heroines Against Guns' hashtag has dominated social media trending patterns for the past two weeks," she said boldly. "I think the rebranding is taking hold."

Hutch waggled his finger at her. "That's all well and good," he chided, "But don't think that gets you off the hook for that Texas debacle. It took a bit of political capital to pull off that conflict between the open carry and anti-gun forces in the first place." He shook his head. "That was supposed to end with more police bodies than it did. I'm still not sure what happened there."

Cheryl was puzzled as well. Three men in that position, with the ordinance at their disposal, should have amassed quite the body count — yet something unforeseen had interfered. It appeared that two of the men had shot each other's arms off, and the third was wounded, and died before he could talk to the authorities. "What's important is that it couldn't be traced back to the movement," Cheryl interjected.

"Yes," Hutch said with mild sternness. "Thanks to the cleanup crew that I contracted." His countenance then softened. "Oh, don't get me wrong, dear," he said. "It was a good plan, and your heart was in the right place. But I think your strengths lie more with school shootings. The victims create more sympathy for your cause." He chuckled warmly, "And they're less likely to shoot back."

The folks seated around the table joined him in laughing at his joke, except for Cheryl. She took her seat, cheeks crimson with embarrassment. She promised herself she would stage the mother of all school shootings. She just needed to find a really disturbed toddler in a Christian preschool.

"Each of you has come up with good plans," Hutch continued. "Mr. Ehrlichman has rewritten the rules of journalism with his online broadcasts. And Reverend Bluntman is the undisputed master of using race as a bludgeon against the traditional forces of law and order."

"Resist, we munch," Hal Bluntman sputtered in his trademark combination of incoherence and moral turpitude. "And must we munch persist."

"Exactly as you say," Hutch smiled. "But we still have a lot to do. We all want this country to be a better place, but there are so few who can appreciate the scope of our overall vision. For generations, much of the country has been…inoculated against our ideas."

"Anti-buddies, to desist inflection," said Bluntman, sagely. "We have much desistance in our neighborhoods. It has given them impunity to change." He nodded confidently, as if he had just made plain to all what they were struggling to understand before.

"That's right," Pummel said. "Well, I'm happy to tell you today that your combined efforts are having the desired effect."

He turned toward the wall behind him, where a flat screen television was mounted. He aimed the remote control at it,

and it flickered to life, showing a street stampede of young people wearing bandana masks, looking like bank robbers from an old-time western film.

"Ah, the heroic Fascist Fighters," Ehrlichman sighed. "I'm a huge fan. Are they going to be joining us?" he asked hopefully.

"No," Pummel said, his avuncular smile unwavering. "No, they're not joining us. They're already with us. They just don't know it yet."

The scene changed to a monument of a Confederate war general. "Folks, I believe the key to the next civil war lies, ironically, in the last one."

"Who gets to be the slaves this time around?" Bluntman asked with surprising lucidity.

"Not to worry, Reverend," Hutch said. "Our friends here are very angry over the idea of remembering the so-called 'War Between the States.' They've had their discontentment and disenfranchisement stoked over the last several years, and we've given them a target for their anger: statuary!"

The men and women in attendance nodded, feigning understanding. Knowing that they did not follow him, Pummel continued to explain his plan. The scene shifted to another scene, just as familiar to his audience — men and women carrying American flags and torches. The men wore their hair cropped close on the sides, long on top, and sharply combed over.

"Meet our other friends," he said.

"You can't be serious," Contessa spat. "They're Nazis!"

"Some of them are, yes," Hutch said. "Some of them are, indeed, actual Nazis. But like many of those in the Fascist Fighters, the majority of them are merely activist actors. Oh, don't look so sullen, Mr. Ehrlichman, surely you knew. They're all our actors. And they're going to face off against each other — in the name of preserving a carved piece of rock." He chuckled to himself at the brilliance of the plan, knowing that nobody else understood it.

"Middle Americans, the people who sit at home and watch their televisions and absorb all the discontent — they're the ones who really make a difference. They've been told that all the disturbing images they've endured are protected by their Constitution. The right to free speech. The right to bear arms. The right to assemble. Rights their grandparents would have died — did die, in many cases — to protect. But we've got them rethinking those rights now. Shown the absurd extremes of situations which that archaic document protects, they grow weary of it. This will motivate them to take action when the time is right, to demand a new Constitution, and repeal the old one that has stood in the way of progress for too long."

Pummel clicked the remote he held, and the image on the screen behind him changed to a woman, her expression pious and pitiful as she cradled a pre-teen girl in her arms. The girl was emaciated, her skin sallow, her weak smile forced as she leaned into her mother's caring embrace.

"This is Andrea Carruthers," Pummel said, indicating the woman in the picture. "You've seen her on the news. Her daughter, Lindsay, is suffering from a condition so rare that

medical science hasn't been able to name it, let alone diagnose it. Lindsay will go through periods of remission, only to have sudden relapses that nearly kill her. Andrea's every waking moment is devoted to Lindsay's care. Andrea can do this, because she has the support of her family, her friends — even complete strangers who have been moved enough by her condition to donate money and resources."

Those around the table nodded with recognition. Some of them had almost been moved to give themselves, but chose instead the more reasonable road of support, which involved posting online photographs of themselves holding signs displaying the "#SaveLindsay" slogan.

"What nobody realizes," Pummel said, "is that the cause of Lindsay sickness is none other than her own mother."

He paused to let the notion sink in. Seeing that his point evaded their understanding, he continued.

"It's called *Munchausen by Proxy*," he said. "It is a psychological condition in which a person gets fulfillment through sympathy from others — not for their own misfortune, but for the misfortunes of someone close to them — misfortunes that they secretly cause. It allows them to play the dual roles of both martyr and savior."

He began a slow saunter around the table. "This country needs to be taken in a new direction. This country needs protected from itself. 'All enemies, foreign and domestic' — isn't that how the oath goes?" Hutch paused behind a silent gentleman, their resident Constitutional scholar, and placed his hand on the shoulder. "If we want to get America on our side

— if we want to get the power of the sympathy of the public — we have to take a completely different approach."

Hutch Pummel stopped pacing, stood next to a fringed United States flag, and did what he always did: he delivered a pragmatic solution.

"If we want to make America well," he intoned solemnly, "first we have to make it sick."

CHAPTER
FIVE

THE BILLINGS, MONTANA 'SETTLE INN' WAS NOT a five-star establishment, but it was a far sight better than a no-tell motel. Its few frills included a small meeting room off the side of it for business guests to reserve, which was really just a table, three chairs, and a phone.

That was all Bob Janos needed to screen applicants who had answered his online call for "activists looking to make a difference." If 'making a difference' was not reason enough to volunteer, however, the advertisement also listed a stipend of "$200 in cash, plus free lodging and travel," which was enough to generate a wave of newfound civic engagement.

Bob knew that most of the respondents were just there for the paycheck and the opportunity to see another part of the country, but he still gave each one the same earnest spiel about appreciating their service, how they were helping take their country back, and how it was people like them who taught King George's men a thing or two about what real patriots would do for the country they loved.

The ones that were enthralled by his pitch, he listed in one group. He wanted to keep them together, near the back of the protest, where they would busy themselves talking with each

other about how they were very good people doing a very good thing for their very good country.

Then there were the ones just there for the job. They would hold any sign, chant any slogan, and march any street, so long as money landed in their bank accounts. These he would place in the middle of his ensemble — they would bulk up the head count in photographs, but they would be inaccessible to the media, and would not have to answer questions.

Finally, there were the hardcore believers. They were much like the first group, except they were motivated by something other than patriotism, no matter what they deluded themselves into believing. These were angry, bitter men and women; they were tired of uppity left-wingers, immigrants, minorities, and everyone who was not like them — namely, white.

These he would put in the front of the march, to lead the chants, and to guide the others on their way with lighted torches.

It was a good system, and it never failed to put the right people in the right places.

A knock at the door was followed by a man's voice. "This where we come to get paid to protest?"

Bob Janos looked up from his organized stacks of applications. The man in the doorway was thin and forgettable, despite whatever statement he was trying to make with the tight black t-shirt, black chinos, and Italian loafers. He held a copy of the advertisement and application printed from the Internet.

"You got it," Bob said with practiced cheerfulness. "That is, if y'all are looking to help take our country back —" He took the application from him and read the name. "— Mister Lee?"

"Back to where?" Remo asked flatly.

Middle group, Bob noted to himself, his smile never fading the slightest. "Pay is two hundred, plus travel to Arlington, Virginia and lodging. Sound good to you?"

"What's in Arlington?" Remo asked.

"America's future," Bob replied.

"America's future is a graveyard? I could have told you that." The voice behind Remo Lee was accented, and somewhat musical. Peering around the taller man was a scrawny little Asian whom Bob thought could be knocked over with the breeze from a slamming door, if he did not first crumble into dust. The little man was bald, except for two wisps of gray hair that stuck out from his temples, and a similarly wispy strand that clung to his chin. He had skin like wrinkled parchment, which stood in contrast to the ornate silk kimono that draped over him.

"It will be if we let it continue in the direction it's going," Bob said. "Are you here to join our march?"

"This is my father, Chiun," Remo said. "He's just along for the ride."

"The man said it pays," Chiun interjected.

"Two hundred dollars," Bob repeated.

"American dollars?" Chiun sniffed. "Worthless. Can you pay in gold?"

"I like how you think, Mister Chiun," Bob said. "Our economy has been driven into the ground by our leaders bowing to foreign powers. And those who control our country's wealth, well they're not exactly from our kind of tribe, right?"

Chiun sniffed. "The corruption of currency is older than that," he said dismissively. "Many blame the Greeks and the Persians, and they are not wrong in this understanding — but like most whites, they are shortsighted. The problem truly began with the Egyptians."

"Gold is where the smart people going these days." *True believer*, Bob noted, figuring where best to place the wizened old Asian. "Nothing holds its value like gold."

"Finally, a white who understands," Chiun said to Remo, his eyes brightening.

Remo shook his head. "He's not going," he said again. "I just brought him with me so he didn't burn the house down while I was gone."

"Bring him along," Bob urged him. "The more the merrier, right? Here, take one of these." Bob handed Remo a key card and a slip of paper with a room number and a list of bullet points. "In case someone in the media picks you out of the crowd for an interview, you'll know what to say."

Remo glanced at the sheet and nodded. "Thanks."

Bob dug in a box and pulled out one of many bandanas, printed to look like American flags. "Wear this when we go," he said. "Like the boss, you know?"

Remo let the bandana hang limp from his fingers, and

looked at it with barely disguised chagrin. "Born in the U.S.A." he muttered.

"Mr. Chiun, you sure I can't convince you to sign up with us?" Bob Janos held out another bandana, and Chiun looked at it as though he were being offered a rotted fish, dead seven days.

"Why are you handing me that?" he asked. "Surely you do not wish me to wrap that about my head?"

Bob smirked to himself and gave Chiun another appraising look. "Perhaps something in white?" he countered.

Chiun nodded. "Let us discuss your terms."

Remo shook his head and walked away. The last thing he wanted right now was to be a part of contract negotiations. Chiun would have that guy going in circles in less than ten minutes, come away with triple the fee, and probably some kind of signing bonus, too.

As he rounded the corner, he crumpled the paper and flung it down the hall, sending it neatly into a wastebasket near the elevator.

The tiny act did little to alleviate the edginess that had been plaguing him. For the past several days, Remo had found himself looking for reasons to use Sinanju. Not parlor tricks, either, but the deeply satisfying act of carrying out the business. He had been surprised at how hard it was to accidentally run into people who deserved it, and his frustration had been mounting, like an itch he could not scratch.

He had meant to bring it up to Chiun, but Upstairs had

sent him on another mission so quickly, he had gotten momentarily distracted. The mission had been enough to temporarily assuage him, but he still needed to talk to his master, before the wrong opportunity presented itself.

"Nice shot," a female voice piped up from behind him.

Remo turned to see an elfin face with sparkling blue eyes and blonde hair so straight it appeared to have been ironed into a sheet. She was a head shorter than Remo, with a build like a gymnast. Her short-sleeved white blouse was new enough to still have the original creases, and was tucked into a pair of faded denim shorts that were quickly unraveling into strings at the hems. Against her neck rested a pendant: a red, white and blue enameled Confederate flag.

She extended her hand. "I'm Ewe," she said, pronouncing it like the female sheep.

"I'm pretty sure I'm me," Remo replied, taking her hand.

Ewe rolled her eyes, but smiled. "It's Hawaiian," she said. "It means 'lineage.'"

Remo looked the pale blonde up and down again, checking for any trace of Polynesian, and found none. "Funny," he said. "You don't look Hawaiian."

She giggled and shook her head. "Of course not. But my daddy was stationed in Hawaii when he was in the Navy," she replied. "He saw it in a list of baby names."

"I think they pronounce it 'EH-way,'" he said, knowing they did.

She shook her head again. "I looked it up in the dictionary and it's pronounced 'you.' Of course, the English dictionary

says it's a sheep, but in Hawaiian it means 'lineage.' Daddy said it would remind me I was pure."

"Pure what?" Remo asked.

Ewe giggled. "You're funny. What's your name?"

"Remo Lee," he replied.

She nodded approvingly. "Nice name," she said. She held out her tiny hand. "Ewe Johnson. So, Lee — that's not short for 'Lieber' or 'Liebowitz' or anything, is it?"

"Oh, good heavens, no," Remo replied. "But my mother was a Goldstein."

Ewe's eyes widened, as though she had seen horns grow out of Remo's forehead. "Really?"

"No, I was just kidding," Remo smiled.

The girl relaxed once more. "You shouldn't say things like that," she said, lightly punching his arm. "Some people might get the wrong idea about you."

"Like what? That I'm rich?"

She looked up, searching his eyes for something. The longer she looked, the more she got drawn into them. They were deeply set, and shadowed by his brow. There was something about this man that set the tiny hairs on her body at alert, as though she should run from him as quickly as she could. And yet there was a magnetism as well, that made her feel she might fall into those eyes and become lost.

As she gazed into the abyss, it was gazing into her as well, and it did not like much of what it saw. Sure, Remo could appreciate the pretty packaging, the shapely form of her breasts and the gentle curve of her hips. But Remo could sense

that there was an evil that festered inside her. She might not burn a cross on someone's lawn, but she might set up a stand across the street to sell cups of gasoline to those who would. Yes, there was that kind of evil in her, but not the kind that required the special services of a Master of Sinanju's deadly art.

Of course, not every art of Sinanju was deadly, and Remo could not deny that the girl was deserving of some kind of lesson. Deep inside him, something simmered, and cried out with satisfaction that justice was about to be served.

Ewe blinked. "You're a funny man, Remo Lee," she said, slowly.

"I am hilarious," Remo replied. "Let me show you." He took her hand and, keeping eye contact with the pretty blonde, gently ran a fingertip along her ulnar artery.

"What are you…?"

Ewe's question went unfinished, and would only be answered much later, as she followed Remo to his room.

CHAPTER
SIX

HUTCH PUMMEL KNEW THERE WERE three kinds of people who watched the news. The first, and by far the largest, watched it for the dopamine fix that accompanies confirmation bias. They knew the state of the country, and sought out a network that framed events to fit neatly into their pre-established worldview.

The second group was far smaller. These were people who watched the news to learn what was happening in the world.

The third group was a group of one, and consisted of Hutch Pummel himself. He only watched the news to confirm that the reporting followed the narratives that he had established.

Pacing leisurely in his spacious office, nodding along with the news anchor speaking through the television mounted to his wall. If anyone had been with him in the room, they might have noticed that he was silently mouthing along, just slightly ahead of the serious looking brunette who peered at the camera with what one could easily assume to be utmost concern.

"It's been nearly a month since the tragic events of Little Rock, which saw evil long thought vanquished claim the life of

single mom and hospice volunteer Marissa Meyer," she said, as the image changed to a photo of Marissa, smiling in her graduation cap and gown.

"Now the picture with the baby," Pummel muttered under his breath, as though directing the broadcast.

At his utterance, the photo faded out to be replaced with a slightly older Marissa, standing with her arms in a hug around a young girl whose smile showed everyone she had recently lost her two front teeth. "Marissa was an example of love and compassion, seeking to make a better world, not only for her young daughter Melanie, but for her fellow human beings."

"And the money shot," Pummel whispered.

On cue, the idyllic family photo was replaced with a shot of Roger Whitman's truck wrapped around the tree, Melissa Meyer's upper torso jutting out from above it like a grotesque hood ornament. "But that love and compassion was no shield against the raw, savage hatred shown by neo-Nazi protesters, who find their ideology threatened by attempts to correct the mistakes of America's shameful history." The camera returned to the somber expression of the female anchor. "And still, the only word out of the White House is that there were, and we quote, 'good-hearted folks on both sides.' It's a dark day when a sitting American president can see the 'good heart' in white supremacy. A dark day indeed."

Pummel had heard what he needed to hear. The rest of the hour would be devoted to a panel discussion where the talking points would seed the viewers' minds through repetition without further elaboration.

He switched to another network, where the discussion would appear a bit more confrontational, and thus would be deemed fairer and more balanced.

"The framers of the Constitution were great men." The black man with the graying temples spoke deliberately and evenly. "But to believe that the Constitution protects hate speech is simply not true. Hate speech clearly falls into indefensible categories like defamation, fighting words, and obscenity. The Supreme Court —"

"The Supreme Court," the host interrupted, "has sided every single time that hate speech is protected by the First Amendment, and rightfully so." The host also spoke evenly, yet passionately, his white hair only slightly paler than his skin, which stood out in contrast to the chalkboard behind him, upon which were scrawled names, dates, and connecting lines delineating every hate speech case from *Brandenburg v. Ohio* to *National Socialist Party of America v. Village of Skokie*. The chalkboard had been a staple of the show, one Pummel was rather proud of. It subliminally reminded viewers of their days in school, and thus silently imbued the host with the authority of a teacher, someone to be heeded.

"The Supreme Court also decided that Dred Scott wasn't an American citizen because he was of African ancestry," his guest countered.

"That doesn't have any bearing on these cases," the host parried.

"It proves the Supreme Court can be wrong. Or maybe you think they were right then, too?"

The discussion devolved into a shouting match right on schedule, and Pummel turned off the set. Everything, so far, was following a meticulous plan that had been years in the making. The media was doing its part to stoke the fires that would infect the apathetic, forcing them to take sides. By morning, respected online polls would show a majority of Americans agreed that the Supreme Court was wrong. The data was already being cultivated and assembled.

Hutch Pummel slowly ambled a lap around the centerpiece of his office, an ornately carved wooden desk barren of any decoration or device, save for a phone and a laptop computer. He settled into the plush chair behind the desk and clicked a link, opening a private, encrypted video chat.

A window opened on the screen, showing a man in his late thirties who was trying, and failing, to hold onto his twenties. He was balding in front, but sported a man-bun in the back. In the photo that appeared on Hutch Pummel's screen, he was in mid-sip from a coffee mug that obscured the lower half of his face. He peered over it through square-framed glasses, and his cheeks bore a patchy beard that desperately needed a trim. A cat perched on his shoulder as though it owned him.

A nasal, reedy voice came through the speakers of Pummel's device. "Damn it, everything's lagging. Stupid freaking hotel wi-fi. He's going to be on any minute, and I can't even — oh, now it connects. Finally."

"Hello, Mister Lafferty," Pummel said calmly. "So glad you were able to take my call." Hutch Pummel knew that on Craig Lafferty's end, the screen displayed nothing but black, just as

he knew his voice was being triple-modulated so that it would sound nothing like his real voice.

"Oh, you're there," Lafferty said, dropping his voice half-an-octave. "No problem, no problem. Happy to help any way I can. Punch Nazis. Kick fascists. Whatever it takes, right?"

Pummel smiled to himself at the enthusiasm on display. It used to amaze him how easily it was to find a pawn to perform the most questionable of acts. Now, he would be surprised if he could not find someone to do his bidding.

"I'm so glad you feel that way, Mr. Lafferty," he said warmly. "But it's your engineering skills I'd like to employ for this particular venture. Particularly your more, shall we say…eruptive talents?"

"Right, right," Lafferty responded. "I don't know why people haven't taken it on themselves to blow up these concrete atrocities already. You name it, I'll blow it! Uh, I mean blow it *up*. Blow it sky high."

"Sky high is good," Pummel said, stifling a chuckle. "But any fool with enough dynamite can do that. No, Mr. Lafferty, I'm not all that enthused about how the target goes up. But I'm much more interested in how it comes down."

For the next few moments, Pummel laid out in painstaking detail exactly what he had in mind for Craig Lafferty's talents, receiving several eager assurances that it would be no problem at all.

"Easy as pie," Lafferty said. "I just need early access to the target so I can calculate the proper forces, angles, and azimuth."

"Access won't be a problem," Pummel assured him. Then he added with a tone calculated to stoke the man's ego. "We're all counting on you to get this right, son. This will be our Lexington, our Fort Sumter. You're going to make history."

Pummel was sure he heard the sniffle of tears coming from Lafferty's end. "You can count on me, sir," Lafferty choked out. Pummel could picture the former Army demolition expert, now hipster, saluting his monitor, and smiled as he closed the connection.

By the end of the week, Hutch thought, America would have be sick to death of its Constitutional freedoms, and America would finally be in position to get the President it deserved.

CHAPTER SEVEN

REMO WILLIAMS WAS CONFLICTED as he pulled the tight black t-shirt down over his lean torso. On one hand, he felt calm and relaxed, the nagging voice of need now silenced for the time being. On the other, he felt guilty for indulging his urges. It was like being thirteen all over again, and he hated it.

He looked with mild disgust at the white blouse, denim cutoffs, and lace panties that had been thrown haphazardly around the floor of the hotel room. Their owner was daydreaming in the shower, where the water had been running for nearly twenty minutes. Remo would have gone in and checked on Ewe, but there was no need. One did not need senses honed by Sinanju to hear the tuneless, contented humming of the nimble blonde doll, and stepping into the bathroom with her would only result in her throwing herself at him again for more.

"Two steps more, I wouldn't have this problem," Remo grumbled to himself. The thirty-seven steps to bring a woman to sexual ecstasy were named with a sense of gross understatement. Ecstasy was surpassed while still within the first ten steps. There was a sound reason why such a practice was a tool of the world's most accomplished assassins. The

thirty-sixth step usually brought about insanity in all but the already insatiable, as the lateral orbitofrontal cortex underwent a complete shutdown. With the thirty-seventh, the amygdala popped like a balloon.

Still, as problems go, he had to admit this one at least came in a pretty package. And she was just a few feet away, her skin still shiny and soapy…

Remo shook his head to clear out the cobwebs. He definitely needed to sit down with Chiun and figure out what was going wrong with him. This one particular detail, however, he might leave out.

A gentle rap at the door was followed by it opening to admit the Master Emeritus of Sinanju, his eyes narrowed to slits of vellum as he smiled with unadulterated joy. Remo took one look at him and groaned.

"Look, Remo," Chiun declared. "Not only was I able to negotiate a rate four-fold of the initial offering, but the observant Mister Janos even gifted me with this white kimono of purity."

"Chiun, that's not a kimono."

"Oh, I know that, but I did not wish to insult the giver of the gift by pointing out his ignorance," Chiun replied. "After all, he is only a poor white and cannot be held responsible for his lack of knowledge, being no doubt a product of what passes for education in your so-called United States of America. And besides, he also presented me with reverential headgear." Here, the wizened Korean master produced a rolled-up cotton hood that unfurled into a vaguely triangular

shape. He placed the conical hood upon his bald head such that his face peered out the open side while the rest draped about his nape and ears.

Remo sighed and pinched the bridge of his nose. "Chiun, does any of what you're wearing look even slightly familiar to you?"

The old master folded his arms and beamed at Remo. "Of course it does," he said. "The headgear is very clearly an indication that Mister Janos believes I should hold a place of high honor, as it bears a nearly identical resemblance to the that worn by the leader of your carpenter's cult. The kimono may require some modest alterations, as it is too funereal in its current form, but again one cannot fault Mister Janos's empty brain when held in balance with his full heart."

"Chiun," Remo started. "This is a KKK hood and robe."

Chiun stood unfazed. "Do not exaggerate, Remo," he said. "It is slightly large, but not grossly so."

"KKK isn't a tag size," Remo moaned. "It's a group of people, if you can call them that, who think that blacks, Catholics, and Jews are inferior."

The Master Emeritus remained unmoved. "As I have told you myself, many times."

"They're not too crazy about Asians, either."

"Nor am I," Chiun replied.

"Including Koreans."

"Most Koreans deserve their scorn."

Remo centered himself and tried to find the words that would resonate with the stubborn old man, and then snapped

his fingers. "They believe that whites are superior to everyone else."

But even at this, Chiun merely shrugged. "Nobody is perfect," he replied beatifically. "Except of course for the exalted personage of Chiun."

"Look," Remo said, an edge of aggravation in his tone. "I don't care how grateful you are for this 'gift,' or how honored you are to have it — but you are simply *not* going to go out wearing this thing."

Chiun drew himself up to his full height. His cheeks trembled and darkened. "Always it is so with you," he spat. "'Chiun, you cannot kill the man mowing during your naptime.' 'Chiun, you cannot drive the car.' 'Chiun, you cannot grow dogs for their meat.' Who are you to tell a Master of Sinanju what he can or cannot do? I have been the Master far longer than you, and my knowledge and experiences are deeper and vaster than you should ever accomplish alone. But does this enter your thinking when you observe me? No. You see a doddering old man who must be prevented from soiling his adult diapers, and have food dabbed from his chin."

Remo sighed. "Little Father," he said, in a more deferential manner, "people will look at you and get the wrong idea. They'll mock you. They'll revile you."

Chiun cocked his head. "Do you think I do not know how to respond to such nonsense, or that I even care about it?"

"I care about it," Remo said. "When it's directed at you."

The old man's eyes softened. "You really believe I look so ridiculous, my son?"

"Not you," Remo said carefully. "Just that outfit."

Chiun nodded. "Very well," he said. "If you are that sure that I would draw disrespect adorned as such, I shall —"

At that moment, the bathroom door opened, and out stepped a very bubbly and very naked Ewe Johnson. She smiled exuberantly at Remo, and strode quickly toward him, barely noticing Chiun until her hands were on Remo's shoulder and her right leg was drawn up against his. When she did notice the old man, Remo immediately wished he had finished the job on her.

Shoulders sagging, Remo meekly introduced the girl as she unabashedly stood there. "Chiun, this is Ewe."

Chiun raised an eyebrow. "I assure you, it is not."

"Oh my god," she said, noticing Chiun for the first time. "I love your outfit! You look absolutely amazing!"

Remo rolled his eyes, as Chiun gave him a withering stare.

"What did you do," he asked, clipping each word.

"I didn't mean to," Remo replied meekly, as Ewe rubbed her body up against him, purring. "Chiun, we really have to talk. I've been having these needs lately. Like something's changing inside me lately, and…I just don't know what to do about them."

"This is not a new thing," Chiun sniffed. "I know an ancient Sinanju technique that will easily curtail these urges you feel," he said curtly.

"I'm all ears."

"Take a cold shower." The Master turned on his heel and made for the door. "And I am keeping the kimono. It is

'absolutely amazing.'"

He slammed the door, a crack erupting in the jamb like a miniature fault line.

"Well that's just great," Remo grumbled. He stood with his arms crossed, while Ewe stood on her tiptoes and tried to nibble at his ear.

CHAPTER EIGHT

THEY ALSO SERVE WHO ONLY STAND AND WAIT was a mantra drilled into Smith early in his career with the CIA, when he was a much younger man in, as he remembered it, a much simpler time.

While the younger Smith may have desired a more active role at times when he was with The Company, the older Smith knew full well how much was accomplished through information gathering, data collating, pattern matching, psychological profiling, and monitoring the activities of others. All of these important tasks and more had informed his designs when establishing the architecture for the CURE computer systems, a data processor that was two generations ahead of its brothers in the field of national security.

But the system, as good as it was, still had the same weakness as the earliest electronic thinking machines: it needed data to work with. This was the main reason Smith kept Remo in the field — Remo gathered raw data, which Smith would use to feed the beast, so it could churn out information that, more often than not, would prove critical to national security.

The machine was always active, even as it waited for the information Smith was trying to provide: the person who was

stoking the flames of aggression, and trying to drive the country into a new civil war.

Smith's last contact with Remo had disturbed him, but no less than most of his interactions with CURE's enforcement arm. Despite the fact that the conversation was persistently interrupted on Remo's end by the insufferable giggling of a woman Remo had seemingly decided to bed while on assignment, Remo relayed that he had nonetheless met the man organizing the counter-protest group.

A deep search on Bob Janos turned up no prior criminal activity. He was not registered with any political party, he maintained a minimal social media presence, and he worked for no known PAC. He seemed to have organized the demonstrations of his own accord.

Remo had also learned what city would be subjected to the next round of protests. As the groups seemed to focus on monuments to the southern confederacy, the most obvious choice seemed to be the Confederate Memorial in Arlington Cemetery. But northern Virginia was home to a number of other such statues. Smith realized it was possible that Arlington might be nothing more than a meetup location, before protesters mobilized to a different confrontation site.

Smith sat in silence, his lips pursed together so tightly that he looked as if he were sucking on a lemon peel. His sour expression was born of concern and concentration, and had ultimately become his resting countenance. He sat in silent contemplation for several minutes, before the pulsing vibration of the phone in his desk drawer called for his

attention. Smith opened the drawer and lifted the black handset from its cradle.

"They're killing me, Smith!"

"Mr. President," Smith replied, certain the man on the other end was, indeed, not facing the immediate threat of assassination.

"Absolutely killing me," the President continued. "I'm being crucified in the press. I'm being stabbed in the back in the Senate. The House is out for my blood! And the independent counsel is shoving a red-hot poker up my —"

"What can I do for you, Mr. President," Smith asked calmly.

"Give me something I can work with regarding these riots," he replied. "I can't keep tweeting the same stump speech rhetoric every day. Sooner or later, even my base is going to expect results. If even one more person gets killed, I'll be looking down the barrel of impeachment."

Despite the harsh tone directed at him, Smith commiserated with the President's desire for results, and planned to remind Remo during their next scheduled call that he was embedded within the protest group to find out who was pulling the strings that pitted both sides against each other, not to engage in relationships with young women.

"We are still working on that, Mr. President," Smith assured him. "I cannot tell you more than that."

"Will you tell me when you can tell me?" the President asked. "Or will even that be kept top secret?"

"I cannot say, Mr. President."

"Well can I at least tweet out that we have our best guys investigating the matter?"

"I would strongly recommend against that, sir," Smith replied. He did not add that the CURE computer system was already monitoring and intercepting the President's flood of social media communiqués, scrambling them whenever they veered to close to endangering national security.

Just then, Smith's monitor displayed a flashing icon, indicating a situation that the algorithms felt deserved the attention of CURE's Director.

"If you'll excuse me, sir, we may have a new lead even now," Smith said. "Rest assured, I will let you know when a resolution has been achieved, regardless of what it is."

"Fine, fine," the President said. "Just make it quick."

Smith hung up the phone and clicked on the icon, hoping the CURE computer's ever-vigilant processes had put together some of the pieces.

He exhaled, disappointed, as he saw it was information from past cases, and was not related to the crisis at hand. Frequently, CURE assignments would turn up tangents that hinted at further threats to the unity of the country. More often than not, they were cranks, and more easily dealt with by standard agencies, or even local police. A tip in the right place, a nudge in the proper direction, and CURE would never need to get involved. Other times, there might be no threat at all, and the data being processed regarding such events would be archived away — but never deleted, just in case.

Occasionally, archived files would be automatically revisited whenever new bit of information made them

potentially relevant. Information gleaned from the riots in Gateway City, for instance, implicating Reverend Hal Bluntman's involvement in exacerbating crumbling race relations, had been archived in such a way, and the system was notifying Smith that the files were being reactivated due to new connections found.

The connection might have been irrelevant. Only Smith could determine that. In this instance, he was inclined to ignore the alert. True, Hal Bluntman and Cheryl Sparks were both persons of interest in separate incidents, but neither of those seemed to have any connection to the other.

Smith's alert flashed again, showing FAA manifests that revealed that both Bluntman and Sparks had taken flights to Denver International Airport on the same day last week. Smith performed a perfunctory check of the aggregated headlines filtered to Colorado, and saw nothing to indicate a cause for alarm. Still, it was enough to rouse the attention of the most vigilant decision engine on the planet, so Smith opted not to dismiss the correlation and allow the system to compile more data. Smith had learned long ago that even the tiniest flicker of light was enough illumination to expose the darkest of evils.

As his computers continued scouring, Smith resumed his focus on the matter at hand: seeking out the puppet master who was fomenting civil unrest. If the CURE computer found something else worth pursuing, he would see it later.

This time, CURE's computers were already a step ahead of Smith.

CHAPTER NINE

A CARAVAN OF GREYHOUND BUSES filled the parking lot of the Settle Inn, creating an uninviting scene for any families who might otherwise have found the hotel a decent place to stop for the night. If the buses did not discourage visitors, the congregation amassing outside the automatic door certainly would have. Bob Janos was all that stood between the throng of people ready to save history — for a stipend — and the buses that would carry them to glory.

"We're on the right side of history here, folks," he said, raising his voice so everyone could hear him. "These hippies and ultra-liberals and dad-gum social justice warriors, they want to erase our history. They want to do away with anything that hurts their little fee-fees. And are we gonna let 'em?"

Parts of the crowd hollered back "Hell no!" with great exuberance. Others gave a half-hearted response, and shuffled anxiously, ready to sit down for long drive ahead.

Remo stood at the far edge of the lot with Chiun, observing with bemusement. "I wonder how many people would show up to save a statue if they weren't being paid to go?" he asked nobody.

Chiun shrugged. "If they were of Sinanju, and the statues were those in the Monument to the Masters, they should all rise up and meet death gladly in the name of preserving the tribute. But as these are mostly whites and mostly Americans, I would hazard that none of them would get off their couches to save their own grandmothers, save that someone offered them money for the appearance of an effort."

"Speaking of which, when do I pose for my Sinanju statue?" Remo asked. "I want to make sure they get my good side."

"I have been assured that sculpting has already begun," Chiun replied flatly. "I have provided them with photography myself."

"Really?" Remo asked. "When did you sneak a photo of me?"

Chiun smiled thinly. "You were doing a most splendid task," he said. "It was after your training with the Rain of Rice."

"That was a long time ago, Little Father," Remo said, recalling the training maneuver. He had already become proficient at avoiding bullets, but Chiun had insisted this was a basic skill, and said that when Remo truly achieved mastery, he would be able to advance on an army and not be hit. Then he flung a fistful of rice at him, many of which penetrated his upper arm and deltoid. The rest of the afternoon was spent with Chiun plucking them out, one by painful one, while telling him how worthless a student he was.

"Was it the first time or the last time?"

"The last time, of course," Chiun said. "The first time, I was convinced you were going to get yourself killed before the week was out. The last time, you avoided every grain. I was very proud. And so, as you were bent over, and picked up the rice from the floor, I commemorated the moment with a photograph."

"While I was bent over?"

"I wanted to be sure to capture your better side."

"So they're going to sculpt me that way."

"Even so," Chiun nodded. "It was a great moment in your training, fitting for memorialization."

Remo nodded. "Fair enough," he said. "That'll make it easier for generations of Sinanju to come up and kiss my —"

"As I live and breathe, you just keep slipping away from me, Remo Lee!" Ewe had spotted Remo from the crowd that Bob Janos continued to try to work up, and had sprinted over to him, throwing herself against his chest and wrapping her arms around his neck.

"Oh," Remo said, nonplussed. "Ewe. It's you."

"You broke her, you bought her," Chiun chided.

"We're sitting together on the bus, aren't we?" Ewe chattered, with the buoyant energy of a schoolgirl's crush. Her eyes sparkled with anticipation of hours and hours of cramped bliss to be shared.

Chiun turned abruptly to Remo. "What does she speak of, 'bus?' Surely, you do not expect me to ride in one of those metal cattle carriers, do you?"

"Oh, we're going to have *such* fun," Ewe said, giggling and

snuggling up to Remo. "Especially at night when it's dark," she whispered, her grin promising mischief of a carnal variety.

"Loads of fun," Remo said, less enthusiastically. "But you know where we can have the most fun?"

Ewe looked up at him vacantly, expecting this dangerous man to tell her what to do. "Where?" she asked, vibrating with excitement.

Remo leaned in close and whispered. "Back of the bus," he said. "No one can sit behind you and eavesdrop, right?"

"Right," she said, her face beaming with agreement. "All the way in the back."

"Back of the rear bus," Remo amended. "The most private, private place to play around."

Ewe was hopping with glee. "Oh yes, Remo! Yes!"

"I have to take care of the old guy here," Remo said. He winked at the girl. "Can you save our seats?"

She threw herself at him and landed a passionate kiss on his mouth before pulling away. "I'll see you there soon!" she said, then ran full tilt toward the string of buses, pushing people out of her way as she forced herself onto the last bus. Remo almost felt sorry for anyone who might already have claimed the rear bench, although he could not imagine anyone clamoring for it, as it was located next to the door to the chemical toilet.

Chiun gave Remo a disappointed look. "And how are you to take care of 'the old guy,' may I ask?"

Remo grinned. "By getting him one of a pair of first-class

plane tickets, courtesy of Smitty," he said, pulling out his phone.

Less than five minutes later, Remo tucked the phone back into his pocket, looking less than satisfied.

"What is it?" Chiun asked. "Did you fail at the negotiations? I knew I should have stepped in when you went silent."

"No, it's fine, Little Father," Remo said. "We have the tickets. I just have to go talk to Bob one more time."

"To let him know you will not be riding the bus?" Chiun asked. "This would be the courteous thing to do, especially for one who so rightly honored the Master of Sinanju with such fine vestments."

"I don't give a rat's patootie if he knows we're on the bus or not," Remo grunted, as he started back toward the lines of people making their way onto the buses. "I'll be right back."

As he walked, Remo pulled a neatly folded triangle of cloth from his back pocket, unfurling it into the red-white-and-blue bandana given him earlier, which he knotted around his forehead.

He found Bob Janos standing at the door of the lead bus, checking names off a clipboard. "Mr. Lee," he said cheerily, looking up. "I had you on the second bus, but Miss Johnson informed me you had other arrangements." He gave Remo a knowing smirk and a wink.

"About that," Remo said. "I'm afraid I'm going to have to make *other* other arrangements. It's my father. He has a medical appointment we completely forgot."

"Oh?" Bob looked concerned. "I hope he's all right. He was looking so forward to the march."

"Believe me, it's all he talks about," Remo replied. "We wouldn't miss it for the world. We're just going to have to meet up with you there."

"At the march?" Bob asked. "Well, that's a bit of a problem. See, we have what you might call 'a man on the inside' with the protesters who want to tear down our history." He lowered his voice. "We know where to head them off, but if we let out early that we know, they're apt to change their mind and head off in a new direction. You get what I'm saying?"

"Sure, sure," Remo said reassuringly. "You can't trust us not to spill the beans."

"Not on purpose, of course," Bob added quickly.

"Loose lips sink ships," Remo said.

"Exactly," Bob said. "Tell you what I can, do, though." He wrote on the corner of the page, then ripped it off and handed it to Remo. "Here's the hotel where we'll be regrouping. Think you can meet us there? We'll arrive in 4 days."

Remo looked at the address and smiled. "We'll be there," he replied.

CHAPTER
TEN

OFFICALLY, THE WEST WING WAS a well-oiled machine. Every cog ran smoothly in its predestined groove; every crisis was handled with clockwork precision; new information was processed quickly and efficiently. Yet since the new administration had moved in, the press had heard that the day-to-day functions of the Oval Office were in complete disarray, verging on — and sometimes crossing into — complete chaos.

This was true.

What was also true was that it had always been this way.

The world was too messy of a place for the White House ever to follow anything like regular order. The administration had to be fluid, capable of changing at a moment's notice, even if that meant the replacement of key staffers, and abrupt reversals on policy decisions.

Today was one of the chaos days. The more-watched media outlets were running a macabre countdown to the one-month anniversary of Marissa Meyer's death. It was touted as a memorial, but it was hard to dismiss the celebratory feeling that exuded from the news networks' talking heads.

"I bet they've got a cake ordered for the occasion," the President grumbled from behind the Resolute Desk. "A great

big sheet cake with candles and that girl's picture printed out of frosting. The ghouls."

"They're just looking for some sign of leadership on this matter…sir," the most recent Chief of Staff offered.

"What more do they want from me?" the President moaned. "Blood? No matter what I say, these news people, these very fake news people, twist it and edit it and make it into what they want people to think I said. I'm telling you, sometimes I hear myself on the news, and I want to impeach myself!"

"You have to control the narrative, sir," his Chief replied. "Give the people something that can't be spliced or cut."

"You're thinking another rally?" the President asked. "We can do another rally. People tell me all the time how much they love the rallies. They're really popular. Huge."

"Actually, sir, there's an opportunity for something a little more subdued," he replied. "Something somber, to reflect on the moment."

The President raised his head. "What did you have in mind, Bill?"

"It's John, sir," the Chief said, flustered. "It's a special memorial dinner being held by the B'nai B'rith next Monday, on the anniversary. You've been invited to speak, although they don't expect you to attend. They've also invited the VP if you can't make it. I think it's a gold-plated opportunity."

The President steepled his fingers thoughtfully at his chin and nodded. "Right. It's a real opportunity. The Jews, they love me, you know. My daughter's Jewish."

"You could really make clear your stance on the neo-Nazis," John added earnestly. "And the, uh, other extremists."

"Antifa," the President said. "We name the enemy in this administration. Remember that." His words were not said sharply, but there was no doubt in anyone's mind they were pointed. "This is almost too good to be true," he added thoughtfully. "So, who's carrying the event?"

"That's the beauty of it," the Chief of Staff replied. "Nobody."

"Nobody?"

"It's going out live on the Internet," he said. "No editing, no cutting room floor. Pure, unexpurgated content."

"I love the Internet," the President replied. "I'd love to cut out press conferences altogether and just go straight to the people via the Internet all the time."

"Yes, sir," John replied automatically.

"We'll do it," the President said emphatically. "Send Mike a note to be ready. We'll both speak."

John stammered. "Both of you, sir?"

The President raised an eyebrow. "Where is this dinner being held?" he asked. "Kussumukstan?"

"No sir," John laughed. "It's in Arlington. At the Sheraton Pentagon City."

"Practically Washington," the President mused. "Yeah, we'll do it. Both of us. It'll be like the campaign trail all over again. I'll make sure we take plenty of hats."

"Sir, it's not a rally. It's the B'nai B'rith."

"You think we could get some 'Make Patriotism

Fashionable Again' yarmulkes?"

"As your Chief of Staff, I'd say that any political headgear might get in the way of your message, sir."

The President nodded agreement. "Right. The press, really hate those hats." He grinned, because he loved that it was so easy to needle the press with a simple trucker's cap. "Well, never mind the hats. We'll focus on the message. Get Joe in here to take some notes."

"Joe's gone, sir," said the Chief of Staff. "The new speechwriter is Carol."

"Well, get her in here, then," the President said. "We've got to write a speech to end all speeches. Come Monday, there won't be any question as to where I stand on the issues, believe me."

Within five minutes, the Chief of Staff had instructed his secretary to reply on his behalf to the B'nai B'rith that the President and Vice President would both be thrilled to speak at their memorial dinner. Five minutes after that, he informed the Press Secretary, who in turn instructed her aids to draft memos to all the major media outlets, with bullet points designed to inform them of the President's intent, and tease them that they would not be privy to the speech until after it was delivered.

At the B'nai B'rith, Jerome Katz received the welcome news that their memorial was going to be graced by the presence of both leaders of the free world, ensuring their social media presence was going to spike through the roof. Jerome immediately picked up the phone and called his friend

Joe Segal.

"Joe, it's Jerry!" he said. "He's gonna come! Who do you think's gonna come? The President, you boob! Yeah! That was a great idea you had. Me, I didn't think he'd even reply back, but to actually have him here — and the Veep too? I just wanted to say thanks, okay? I gotta run, things are gonna get frantic around here fast. Secret Service is probably gonna want to get everyone's background checked, right?"

Joe congratulated his friend, told him he'd tune in, and that, yes, the Secret Service would probably be very busy with him the next few days.

Hanging up, Joe took out a different phone, with an encrypted digital signal.

His call went unanswered, and Joe was disappointed. He wanted to tell his mysterious benefactor, who had offered him a tidy sum in his bank account just to suggest his friend's memorial idea might benefit from inviting the President to speak, that the suggestion had worked.

But there was no need. Even as he disconnected the call on the phone that would never ring again, every major media outlet was updating their chyrons to let the general public know the President was going speak. Several of the pundits were already assuming what would be said, and were either praising or denouncing it ahead of the actual event.

In his remote mansion in Colorado, Hutch Pummel smiled. The trap was set and the bait was taken. All that was left to do was wait.

CHAPTER ELEVEN

THE FLIGHT FROM Montana to Virginia was an exercise in frustration for Remo. As usual, Chiun found someone who annoyed him, and Remo had to hear a litany of reasons about what made this person a particular irritant, from present-day foibles, to the ancient history of the person's race, and whatever king or emperor had screwed up and caused bad habits to be passed down over generations. This flight, Chiun honed his focus on a slightly overweight German man who sat two seats ahead of them, and who had the audacity to snore while asleep.

"The Hussites would have been successful in their advancement on Prussia, for the House of Sinanju had guaranteed their victory. However, the skinflint named Jan Hus thought our price too steep," Chiun sniffed. "And so they were repelled, and the Polish and the Lithuanians battled futilely, as Prussia retreated into isolation. To survive in the cold mountains, they invented sausage, and were so enamored of their invention they actually codified the proper method of making it. As if there were a right way to prepare the meat of the pig."

"Germans. Sausages. Got it," Remo said, nodding absently.

"No," Chiun said. "Sausage is merely why the slumbering oaf reeks. What matters is the existence of Germany in the first place. Had Jan Hus shown wisdom, and remitted the pittance for the invaluable services of Sinanju, then the territory would have become his. There would have been no war for Kaiser Wilhelm. There would have been no war for Adolph Hitler. So you can see why assassination is the most benevolent of services: it is not for what it does now, but for what it does for future generations."

"Kill Hitler, save the world," Remo mumbled.

Chiun rankled, but turned his attention back to the bald head of the object of his derision. "Tell me again why I cannot have peanuts on this flight."

"They stopped serving peanuts because too many people were allergic to them," Remo said.

"When did that happen?"

"Sometime around the turn of the century, I think," Remo replied. "You don't eat peanuts, anyway."

"I do not wish to eat them," Chiun said. "I simply appreciate their aerodynamic qualities." He held out his palm and pantomimed flicking an invisible peanut from it.

"You want to throw mini-pretzels at him, be my guest," Remo offered.

"Bah," Chiun huffed. "Pretzels do not fly as well. Nor impact as smartly. Heh, heh, heh."

• • •

Arriving at the hotel days before the protest bus, Remo was allowed the luxury of picking his own room — which, it

turned out, was not that much of a luxury in the first place, as all the rooms were the same. He did, however, get the most advantageously-located one, on the top floor, overlooking the parking lot.

With three days before the protesters arrived, Remo had plenty of time to get the lay of the land. After setting Chiun up in his room, hooking the DVD player to the television set, and breaking the shrink-wrap off another season of *As the Planet Revolves*, Remo was free to wander the hotel.

That took all of ten minutes, even at his most leisurely pace. The third floor was all rooms, with an employee lounge across from the elevator. The second floor was an identical layout, with the employee lounge replaced by a coin-operated laundry room. The first floor expanded a little further, as the hotel's front desk, lobby, and common area expanded the hotel's footprint.

Remo had walked a short, slow lap around the lobby, noting how many dining tables and chairs were arranged there, the length of the serving bar, where breakfasts of egg-like product with egg flavoring would be trotted out each morning, and the comically-large do-it-yourself waffle station.

The walk was not calming him. Remo had felt a prickling along his skin since his flight had landed. It was an inexplicable sensation. Remo had seen comic books where the hero would experience a tingling sensation when danger was nearby. *Did he have a Sinanju-sense?*, he wondered with mild amusement. *Probably not.*

A clanging from the kitchen area, followed by a wail mixed

with what might have been a curse, drew him out of introspection.

"Fudgenuggets!"

Turning on his heel, Remo was through the door into the kitchen in three strides. He found a middle-aged fellow in grey coveralls wincing and vigorously massaging the fingertips of his right hand. A refrigerator coil lay on the ground, still vibrating from its drop.

"Mother of pearl, that smarted," the man went on. "Hey there," he said, noticing Remo's presence. "Sorry about that, fella. Got the ends of my darn fingers caught between the bars of this replacement coil, and…" He shook his fingers and grimaced. "Hope I didn't scare you."

Remo relaxed. "You all right?" he asked.

"Eh, I'll be fine," the man replied. "Not my first rodeo. You a guest here, or staff?"

"Guest," Remo said. "So, I probably shouldn't be back here."

The man shrugged noncommittally, turning his palms ceilingward. "The more the merrier," he said. "Name's Simon. Simon Gaylord. I'd shake hands, but it's still sore."

"Remo," Remo said. "You need a hand with that thing?"

"Love one," Simon said. "But I've got another pair in the fridge." He nodded toward the walk-in unit against the back wall, just as the door opened to release a twenty-something woman of mixed ethnicity, which Remo quickly mentally assembled as Mexican and Chinese. Her hair was cut close on one side, with the other a wild bush of gelled spikes dyed neon blue.

"You always keep a girl in your refrigerator, Simon?" Remo joked, taking in the tightly muscled form of the tanned girl.

"Oh no, here we go," Simon said, his eyes closing.

"Ex-CUSE me?" the new arrival said, moving with purposeful strides to Remo. "What did you just call me?"

Remo quickly replayed his words in his head to see if anything he had said rhymed with anything that might be interpreted as insulting. "Uh…'girl?'" he offered tentatively.

"Why the hell are you assuming my gender?" she asked defiantly.

Remo cocked his head. "So you're not a girl?"

"Not right now," she said. "Maybe later. Who knows? Gender's fluid, my dude."

"I stand corrected," Remo said flatly.

"Remo, this is my repair partner. Mei Hernandez, Remo…I don't think I got your last name," Simon said, trying to calm the situation.

"Identity is what you make it," said Mei. "There are infinite combinations of ways to be me."

"And here I thought it was all XX and XY," Remo said.

"Why?" Mei countered.

"Yeah, Y," Remo said. "That's the one that makes a boy a boy. I could always remember it because the Y has the little stick that hangs down from the middle." He dangled his index finger and wiggled it a bit for emphasis.

Mei narrowed her eyes at Remo. "Are you having me on?"

"Wouldn't even dream of it," Remo said, even as he was aware that his pheromone production had involuntarily spiked. *No,* he told himself, *there would not be a repeat of Billings here.*

"I get the feeling you have many sides, Remo," Mei said, stepping much closer. For reasons she could not understand, Mei was drawn to this infuriating stranger. "I have many sides, too."

"So I gather," Remo said. "An infinite combination, if I remember correctly."

She tilted her chin up at Remo. He could see her pulse in the curve of her neck. "Maybe I could show you a few of them," she said. "I can be a girl for a while."

"Uh, Mei?" Simon asked tremulously. "We have to get this coil replaced and get on to the next job."

"The boss is right," Remo said. "Work before pleasure."

"You assume an awful lot," Mei whispered, annoyed. "Simon works for me. Simon, take lunch."

"It's only nine."

"Take a long lunch."

Remo steadied himself, telling himself again that there were better, more productive ways to work out whatever was going haywire inside of him.

Mei wrapped her fingers around his wrist. "Thick wrists," she commented. "Like the rest of you?" She looked up at him with hopeful eyes.

Remo smirked, and let her lead him out of the kitchen.

Simon Gaylord shook his head and picked the refrigerator coil off the floor. "Couple of goony birds, if you ask me," he muttered. "Never saw such a — agh, spacemonkeys!" he cursed again, as the fingertips of his left hand caught in the metal grating.

CHAPTER TWELVE

SIMON GAYLORD WAS FINISHING installing a new coil on the walk-in fridge when he heard the squeak of hydraulics coming from the parking lot. Wiping his hands, he stepped out of the kitchen area to the sight of three tour buses opening their doors, disgorging dozens of passengers, who gathered by the side of the buses as they waited to get their bags.

"Looks like you're going to have a full house tonight," he quipped to the lady managing the desk.

She tapped a few keys on her computer and shrugged. "We still have a lot of rooms left," she said. "We've been busier."

Outside, the drivers were opening the luggage compartments. Simon saw one man, who was balding — yet had enough hair in the back to be knotted into a bun — push his way through the throng toward the front, grabbing a backpack and a duffel and then forcing his way back out.

"Some people got no patience," Simon clucked. "Gotta be the rudest duck in the whole bird pond."

"The what now?" the desk manager asked absently, her focus on the soon-to-be-entering guests. But before Simon could answer, the passengers all began elbowing through the automatic sliding doors, jockeying for position to get their

room keys and a shower.

Everyone except for the rude fellow with the man-bun. He was nowhere to be seen, having set off on foot around the corner and down the street.

Simon Gaylord shrugged, helped himself to a seven-dollar slice of cheesecake and a three-dollar cola from the guest pantry, and enjoyed the rest of his "long lunch," while the desk manager did her best to cope with the deluge of check-ins.

• • •

Craig Lafferty slipped his arms through his backpack and slung his duffel bag over his shoulder. His reservation could wait; he was in no hurry to spend any more time jostling with the mass of pretenders and fakers who were only there to make a quick buck.

Marissa Meyer deserved better than that, and his mission was to see that she got it.

He wanted to reconnoiter the site in advance, in order to assess the best approach. He already had done the preliminary math, calculating the forces and trajectories involved.

Lafferty was an Ammunition Specialist, trained by the U.S. Army. Since entering civilian life, he had grown a patchy beard and a paunch, and somehow had acquired two cats, which were now being looked after by his sister. He could not do twenty pushups these days, or hike twenty miles, but his primary skills were all mental, and as sharp as ever.

The explosives were going to do most the heavy work, anyway.

The twelve-block walk left him panting, and he sat down at a bench to catch his breath. The Moonstags across the street

looked tempting. He was craving a soy latte. *Maybe on the way back*, he promised himself.

Around the corner, he saw the gate, a brown, carved archway inscribed with verse:

> On Fame's Eternal Camping Ground
> Their Silent Tents are Spread
> And Glory Guards with Solemn Round
> The Bivouac of the Dead

Craig Lafferty stroked his whiskers and adjusted his square-rimmed glasses. Then he reached back and unclipped the fake bun from the small ponytail that held it on, and tucked it in his duffel.

Standing straight, he saluted briefly, then made his way through the McClellan gate into Arlington National Cemetery.

Several minutes later, he was at ground zero: the tomb of Moses Ezekiel, Lieutenant Harry C. Marmaduke, Captain John M. Hickey, and Brigadier General Marcus J. Wright.

As far as Lafferty was concerned, the thirty-two-foot tall Confederate Memorial was a blight on the nation. It praised the efforts of the racists and white supremacists who had taken root in this great country, and who had been given safe harbor to come out of the shadows by a President who would never have been elected if the popular vote had been followed, like it should have been.

One person, one vote. That only made sense, and everyone wins.

Lafferty began circling the monument, drawing detailed diagrams of its angles, carvings, and protuberances. He made particular note of the monument's northeastern base, where he would be planting his most critical charges. The explosives in this quadrant would ensure that the monument wasn't just blasted to smithereens, but was instead launched into American history.

"Isn't it lovely?"

Lafferty turned sharply, surprised by the sudden appearance of an elderly lady beside him. She was ninety if she was a day; hell, she may have known some of the Confederate soldiers buried in concentric circles around the memorial.

"It had a good artist," Lafferty conceded. Even if he didn't care for the subject matter, Moses Ezekiel's carving of the gods of war was exquisite.

"All those brave boys, gone so tragically," she croaked out in a refined southern lilt. The hand on her cane quavered as she craned her neck to look up at the reliefs carved into the sides.

He smirked. "Bit ironic, if you ask me," he said. "It's not often that those who betray their country are remembered so fondly."

She looked at him as though he had farted in church. She set her lips in a thin line. "Well, bless your heart," she said softly.

Lafferty's cheeks heated up. Even he knew what that meant under these circumstances. To show how little he cared, he squatted down to take an irreverent seat on one of the

surrounding tombstones, only to leap back to his feet with a yelp.

The dowager chuckled. "That's why all the Confederate markers have points on the top," she drawled. "To keep damned Yankees from sitting on them." She turned and hobbled away, her shoulders shaking with a very satisfied laugh.

Lafferty fumed. *The sooner he could rid the world of this reminder of the past, the better*, he thought. It was going to take a few nights to plant that many explosives, and he would have to be extremely vigilant to avoid being seen, but his benefactor had informed him where he could hide out, and substantial windows of opportunity would be afforded by the night guards' schedule of rounds.

He would start tonight. Come the night of the march, everyone would see a spectacle they could tell to their grandchildren.

Well, the ones who survived the blast, anyway.

CHAPTER THIRTEEN

"I FLIP WHEN A FELLOW SENDS ME FLOWERS..."

Remo sat on the edge of the bed, head in hands. Apparently, Mei was not just tightly packaged and easily triggered — she also repressed a desire for a career as a lounge singer. Now freed of any and all repressions, she had no compunctions about letting loose in the shower with show tunes. *"I drool over dresses made of lace..."*

"Hey, honey, isn't your guy going to be looking for you soon?" Remo asked, hoping she would realize how much time had gone by since she left the refrigerator repair business for a long lunch that was now encroaching on the dinner hour.

"You're my only guy, Remo," Mei called sweetly from under the running water. *"I talk on the telephone for hours, with a pound and a half of cream upon my face!"*

So much for fluidity, Remo thought. Mei was enjoying being a girl for now. *A few steps of the art had brought some much-needed clarity to her life*, he rationalized. Still, there had to be a better outlet.

"Next time I'm just going to *have* to kill somebody," he muttered to himself.

"What's that, Remo sweetie?"

"The time," he said, more loudly. "I'm going to have to tell

somebody where I am." He moved toward the door and into the hallway faster than she could respond. Standing by his door was Chiun, his arms folded. To anyone else, it might have appeared the old, withered Korean might have fallen asleep standing up. Remo felt the blood rise to his cheeks. "Chiun, how long have you been standing there?"

"Since long before the Hammers and Rogerstein revival began," he replied sadly. "I would have knocked, but you know I am loath to interrupt you when you are training."

"I wasn't...I mean, technically I was, but..."

Chiun raised his hand, stopping him. "You were training," he said flatly, and turned to walk away.

"Chiun, I..."

"Training!" he insisted, his back to Remo, a bony finger stabbed skyward. "But, perhaps, work more on keeping your elbow straight. This is of much more importance for a Sinanju master."

Remo sighed. Talking to Chiun was not going to be as easy as he had hoped, and he certainly was not helping himself any.

"Definitely killing someone next time," he said.

• • •

The lobby was a bustle of activity. Every table was full, and the guests were chatting and helping themselves to the complimentary beer and wine.

"What happened to Refrigerator Guy?" Remo asked the young black lady behind the front desk. "Gaylord something-or-other?"

The young black girl at the counter shrugged. "Beats me," she said. "He said something about making a call and coming

back later, but I got so busy checking in these buses that I lost track of him."

"Buses?" Remo asked.

She nodded toward the crowd mingling in the common area. "All these folks," she said. "They didn't even call in advance."

Remo surveyed the crowd. They were a mixed lot, but they all came together. He could see the cliques forming: the normal people, the apathetic and antisocial people, the tight-knit knots of people whispering about marches, signs, punching Nazis…

"Hey." He glanced at the desk clerk's name badge. "Marquisha. Do you have any reservations for another load about this size, in about two or three days?"

Marquisha tapped the keyboard. "Nope. We don't have any group reservations until later next month."

"You may want to buckle up," Remo said. His eye caught a figure in the back of the room, going from table to table, checking on each little group and couple. "Call it a hunch, but I think you'll probably be full to capacity very soon."

Reaching into the pocket of his black chinos, Remo pulled out the star-spangled bandana and knotted it about his forehead, as he walked toward the man who looked identical to Bob Janos — identical to anyone but a Master of Sinanju.

Two twins leading two sets of protesters fit with Smitty's theory of someone playing both sides of the riots. Now that Remo had this bit of information, he felt one step closer to endgame.

"Mr. Janos," Remo said, approaching the man, hand extended.

Tom Janos smiled. "I told you," he said. "Call me Tom." Then he looked more suspiciously at Remo. "We...did meet, didn't we?"

"Remo!" Mei Hernandez literally skipped over to him and wrapped her arms around his bicep. "You left me! Oh! They're here already! I mean..." She dropped her voice to a whisper and leaned in toward Tom Janos. "You guys are here for the march, right?"

Tom smiled and winked. "You must be Mx. Hernandez," he said, blending the words 'Mister' and 'Miss' with a sort of buzzing Russian accent.

"Just 'Miss' right now," Mei giggled. "Oh Remo, it's going to be so exciting! I'm going to actually fight Nazis and white supremacists!"

"Shh." Tom Janos put a finger to his lips.

"Oh. Right," she said, and quieted. "I signed up to join their march online," she told Remo. "I was going to fly to Houston to join them, but then I found out they were going to be coming here, so..." She let go of Remo and gave a spin and flourish. "Here I am! Oh, Remo, you will join us, won't you? Please say you will!"

Remo looked from Mei to Tom, and shrugged. "Hey, I'm down with punching Nazis if you'll have me," he said. "It's not like I have anything better to do anyway."

Tom Janos looked Remo over appraisingly. "What's your opinion on hate speech?"

"I don't like it."

"Hate crimes?"

"I definitely hate crime."

"Hate groups?"

Remo smirked. "I hate groups worst of all," he said.

Tom Janos tapped his pencil on the clipboard he carried. "I don't know," he said. "We don't really have any more slots in our group."

"Are we joining this group?" The singsong voice of Chiun made Mei jump, so silently had he slipped up behind them. He wore a black kimono, threaded with metallic red silk that made the lower portion seem to shimmer with crimson flames.

"They won't let us in, Little Father," Remo said.

"This is your father?" Tom asked, suddenly interested.

"On my father's side," Remo said.

Tom's attitude underwent a metamorphosis from concern to great appreciation. So many demographics in one little old man. *He would be great optics*, Tom thought, *if he got in front of a camera.*

"Oh, what the heck," he said, enthusiastically. "The more the merrier, right? Can't have too many hands in the fight against fascism, after all." He pointed up to the bandana around Remo's forehead. "You mind wearing that differently?"

Remo cocked his head. "What, like, tied around my leg or something?"

Tom Janos chuckled. "No, like this." He reached up and tugged the bandana down Remo's face, unfurling it as he did until it hung down, covering Remo's nose and mouth like an old-time bank robber. "Perfect," Tom said. "Just for the march, mind you. And as for you, Mister…Chiun, was it? You'd look very respectful in a Guy Fawkes mask."

"And why should I wish to look like a white?" Chiun asked, his eyes glinting dangerously.

"Good point, good point," Tom said, backing off. *Hates whites*, he noted mentally. *Definitely get him in front of a camera.* "Maybe some traditional Asian attire?"

Chiun sniffed and looked down at his kimono, then back up at Tom.

"Right, right," Tom said. "Looks like you've got it all covered, Mister Chiun." He took out his pencil and clipboard. "So that's Mister Chiun and...?" He looked up at Remo.

"Remo," he said. "Remo Grant."

"Great," Tom said, jotting the names down. "So, the counter-protest is three days out. Remember to keep this quiet, and try not to get arrested or anything until then, okay?"

Remo was about to ask where the march would be held, but Tom Janos was already moving on to the next group, carefully shepherding each of them, keeping tabs and making sure they were happy and content. "Three days until we counter-protest what?" he muttered to himself.

"The memorial, silly," Mei giggled.

He looked down at the young girl with the mop of blue hair. "Of course," he said. He took her wrist and softly stroked along her ulna. "But remind me."

Mei shivered. "The white supremacists," she cooed. "The ones who killed Marissa Meyer. They're coming here to protest the removal of the Confederate Memorial."

Remo stopped. "The one in Arlington Cemetery?" he asked.

She looked up at him, doe-eyed. "Of course," she said.

"Who wants it removed?"

"We do, naturally," she said.

"Very wise," Chiun said.

"Chiun," Remo said.

"What?" Chiun responded. "It is an ugly piece of stone, crudely carved with idols of Greek cults."

"He gets it," Mci smiled. "And we want it gone."

Chiun nodded. "Then I must finish preparing for this parade," he said, walking away from them. "The Master must look magnificent when appearing in public, even if only before a crowd of whites."

Remo groaned, then looked at Mei. "Hey, if we want it gone, doesn't that mean the other guys are really the counter-protesters?"

"Of course not, silly," she leaned into him, pressing her body against his. "We're doing the right thing, and they're protesting us doing it. But we're on the right side of history. Good guys always win, don't they?"

"Usually," Remo said. "Sweetie, why don't you go get yourself a drink? I need to make a phone call and let my mother know where I'm staying."

• • •

"Twins," Remo said. "Bob and Tom Janos."

"Assuming that is their real names," Smith replied tersely into the phone. In his Rye offices, he was already initiating a search on Tom Janos, bitterly concerned that his earlier searches on Bob Janos did not disclose this important bit of information.

The pulsing icon in the corner of the screen began to

flicker and turn crimson. Smith winced. The reminder that the CURE computer was directing attention to a connection made between Hal Bluntman and Cheryl Sparks was not an annoyance he wanted at this moment. But the color change meant something had changed, and the situation was now a critical priority.

He clicked the icon, and the computer displayed the earlier information, noting Bluntman and Sparks' recent flights. Added to this were two other flight manifests. One flight carried Bob Janos; the other carried Tom.

Smith pursed his lips so tightly they disappeared into a thin line. As he tapped and clicked on new leads the CURE computer digitally unearthed, more and more flight manifests began appearing, showing the unobtrusive arrival of many well-known political and media figures, including former-sportscaster-turned-political-blogger Kirk Ehrlichman, and feminist march organizer Contessa Shilling.

Smith performed deeper searches, looking for speaking venues, organizing events, anything that might be justifiable reason for these disconnected people to suddenly appear in the same area at the same time.

He saw nothing.

"You still there, Smitty?"

"Yes, Remo," Smith said acidly. "I am always here. If these patterns are correct, I may be close to locating the source of the recent social unrest."

"I hope that means you're finding the bad guy," Remo said. He absently began rotating his free wrist, like a runner stretching before a sprint.

"That is precisely what I mean," Smith replied. "Remo, I want you to stay close to this Tom Janos person. He may let something slip that could be useful."

"No problem there," Remo said. "The guy likes to stay close to everyone who volunteers for him. But I do have one question."

"What is that, Remo?"

"Who do I stick close to when his twin brother shows up?"

CHAPTER FOURTEEN

TWO DAYS later, the lead story of every major news show focused on Arlington, Virginia.

One particular network delivered the news in unusually high dudgeon. "The vandal forces of the so-called Fascist Fighters are on the march once more. These veiled communist thugs are trying desperately to take all that is great in American history, all that has made us the nation we are today, and grind it into the dirt."

Shane Vanity loved being a guest on morning news shows. He found them to be a perfect proving ground, where he could test which lines worked and which did not, in order to further refine his opening monologue for his eponymous nightly show. "If it wasn't bad enough that these — and let's just call them what they are, domestic terrorists — these *domestic terrorists* have destroyed some of our nation's most beloved relics all over the country, now they want to bring their vile, violent fervor to some of America's most sacred ground — Arlington National Cemetery."

"One would think that protest marches wouldn't be allowed on the premises," the blonde-haired co-lead in the tight black dress opined, repeating the prompt coming from her producer through her earpiece.

"Hey, it's government property," Shane said. "Which makes it the people's property, so it's fair game. They got the permits approved, every i dotted, every t crossed, so there's nothing to stand in their way, at least not *legally*."

"You sound like you know something there, Shane," she replied with a sly smile.

Shane Vanity's grin spread across his broad face. "Well, I don't mean that they should be stopped *illegally*, either," he said. "Let me be very clear about that. But if they can get a permit to protest, then it creates a precedent to get a permit for a counter-protest. And that's exactly what a brave group of patriots have planned to save our country's heritage."

"Brave indeed," she said. "The Fascist Fighters have been known to be a very violent crowd."

• • •

"These Nazis have been known to be a very violent crowd, and it's all because of this bastard white supremacist in the White House!"

Sitting before a cardboard backdrop of a brick wall, Kirk Ehrlichman shouted into his computer, his live-stream broadcast going out over the Internet to tens of listeners. Hundreds more would catch the video on replays, and then social media sharing would take it from there. "If not for these heroic Fascist Fighters, we'd all be wearing flashes on our lapels and marched toward the ovens. Make no mistake, that's what this xenophobic, homophobic, afrophobic, Islamophobic, Hispanophobic President wants for you — mark my words! He's a fear peddler!" Kirk sputtered into his microphone, popping the 'p' in 'peddler' so that it his sound

levels spiked. Not that he ever checked his sound levels — he never had to. It was someone else's job. All he had to do was come in, sit down, and talk. Now that he was no longer employed in the sports industry, he could now wax eloquent about his true passion: hating the current President.

"And now, as real patriots take to the streets to protest the symbols of hatred and oppression and systemic racism that pervade every darkened corner of this administration, the emboldened racists and misogynists have risen from the ash heap of history to once again normalize their hatred and bigotry and overall *whiteness*." Ehrlichman glared into the webcam over his glasses, pushing his bushy eyebrows together until they became one. "This patriot can only hope that the eyes of justice look down upon our brothers and sisters as they put their lives on the line — literally, as Marissa Meyer would tell you — to protect this country from the fascists we've found ourselves resisting."

• • •

Smith was fed all the interviews via automated transcriptions generated by the CURE computer. It was faster for him to read ahead than to pick out the information between the layers of bloviating and posturing, to glean the ten percent of fact from the ninety percent of opinion.

The facts about the permits were correct. They were legally obtained. But absent from the broadcasts was the permits' timing: for both parties involved, the papers were turned around with unbelievable speed. Furthermore, the permits were issued within hours of each other. An investigative reporter worth his salt might have taken this as a clue that the

two sides were colluding together for a media show, Smith thought.

Smith knew for certain this was the case, and was busily programming new parameters into the CURE systems, to determine any further intersections between the persons of interest — anything that might reveal the nexus that united them all.

Suddenly, a report came through that set Smith's teeth on edge. He read the report again, then a third time. Making sure the dates and places were correct, he opened the desk drawer and picked up the phone.

It answered on the first ring.

"Tell me you've fixed this thing, Smith."

"Mister President," Smith responded. "You cannot attend this memorial service."

"What? Are you kidding me?" the President asked. "Of course I'm going. I have to go."

Smith expected resistance to his entreaty. "Mister President, we believe an assassination attempt is likely."

"What?", bellowed the voice on the other end. "On who?"

"On you, sir."

A long moment of silence passed before the President spoke again. "My God, you're serious, aren't you?"

"Always, Mister President."

"What makes you think someone's going to try to kill me?"

"I don't think it's a coincidence that the dinner is happening the same day as the Arlington protests," Smith said. "The fact that it is less than a mile away cannot be ignored."

"Well, that's what I have Secret Service for," the President

responded. "Do you have any idea who the potential killer might be?"

Smith struggled to answer. Though CURE's computers were coming up with leads, he still could not state with certainty who was manipulating events.

He knew that it had to be someone powerful — someone who could pull strings with permits, fund protests, and direct media attention. But even if he knew who that person was, it was almost certain that he would not be the man on site to harm the President.

Now Smith had at least two people to find — and possibly more.

"Not at this time, Mister President," Smith replied ruefully.

"Then we really don't know there's any chance of an attack at all," the President said.

"I think it's a near-certainty there will be an attempt, sir," Smith said with surety.

The President gave it some thought. "Okay, Smith," he said. "You've been a solid guy before, so I'll believe you."

"Thank you, Mister President."

"I'll double the security detail."

"Sir, that is not what I was hoping for."

"I'm going to the dinner," the President assured him. "The country needs this. Hell, I need this! If I don't do something to course correct, I can forget a second term. Shoot, if I don't go, they won't even let me finish this one."

"I just want to see you survive your term, Mister President," Smith replied.

"That makes two of us," the President said. "So you know

what you have to do."

"Sir?"

"Don't let me get killed."

The call terminated, and Smith closed the drawer.

• • •

"An assassin," Remo said quietly into the phone. "You're sure?"

"No, I am not sure, Remo," Smith replied. In fact, uncertainty gnawed at his gut, flooding him with indigestion. Smith absently reached for his ever-reliable bottle of Pepto Bismol.

Remo had never let him down in the field before, but this time he was up against an idea, one that was being weaponized in order to bring America to its knees.

How could one man fight against an idea?

"But I also do not believe in coincidence," Smith continued, wiping his slightly pink lips with a handkerchief.

"I'm not big on that either," Remo said. "Okay. I'll go mingle and see what I can suss out. Oh, crap."

Through the phone, Smith heard the high-octave squeal of a woman's voice. "*Remo! Oh. My. God. I missed you sooo much! What happened to you?*"

"Smitty, I have to go," Remo said.

"Remo, what is going on?"

"Let's just say the mingling got a lot more minglier," he replied. "The other team just pulled into town."

CHAPTER
FIFTEEN

AT 10:45 P.M., CRAIG LAFFERTY tucked his shovel and bag under a nearby bush, then crawled in after it, as he had done for the past two nights. At 10:50, he heard the muffled footsteps of the night watchman on his latest trip around the cemetery. By 11:00, Craig would shimmy out once again, covered in dirt and with dry leaves stuck in his beard. He would have another two hours to dig around the base of the monument and plant more charges before he would have to do the whole hide-and-seek thing all over again, before slipping out in the morning to get some sleep.

He wiped the sweat from his forehead with a dirty sleeve, knocking his glasses askew. He envied the other marchers, who had nothing to do all day but take in the tourist attractions of the town. But they were not as important as he was. Any one of them would blow their finger off with a firecracker, never mind C4 charges.

Craig took out his smart phone, the compass app already pulled up. The charges had to be planted in just the right locations, and in just the right quantities, if the explosion was going to blow the monument out of the ground. It was still a lot of C4. Fortunately for Craig, every night he slipped in to

work, he found another duffel bag of it, hidden exactly where he was told it would be. It was good to have friends in high places, the same friends who knew the routes of the night guards, and who paid for his room and meals. And lattes. Staying up all night to plant charges took a lot of soy lattes.

Craig's fingers trembled from the lack of sleep and the overload of caffeine. *I'm fine*, he told himself. Shaky or not, he was too well-trained to mishandle explosives and accidentally set them off.

He dropped a packet of C4, gasped and caught it quickly, juggled it up into the air in a high arc, then gently caught it with both hands cupped to his chest. His heart pounded. He needed something to steady his nerves, and went back to his bush where he had stashed two drink carriers of "yumbo" soy lattes, a word that meant "extra large" in neither Italian nor English. They were cold, but that did not matter to a real man.

Draining the cup in one swig, Craig felt alertness flood his body once more. He flexed his fingers into fists repeatedly until he was sure the jitters had passed. Then he went back to digging and planting. *Only one more night to go*, he thought, pushing aside feelings of panic about how much was left to do.

Craig began humming a happy tune to himself, stopping himself after remembering he was supposed to be quiet. *Music could wait for another night.*

After this was over, they'd be writing songs to Craig Lafferty. He was going to be the American Guy Fawkes.

He might even get his own date on the calendar.

They'll remember me for centuries, he told himself smugly. *Craig*

Lafferty Day. Patriot Day. America's (re)birthday. The day America became a free country again.

• • •

"Can't we all just get along?"

The hotel was fairly big, but once Ewe Johnson arrived it was nowhere nearly big enough. As the latest spate of visitors flowed through the doors into the hotel lobby, Ewe saw Remo through the windows and stiff-armed a middle-aged lady, as she plowed through the crowd, squealing his name.

Remo put away the phone and put on a smile. "Hey, you!"

"You remembered my name!" Ewe cried, jumping into his arms and wrapping her legs around his waist. "Oh my God, I *missed* you! I thought I'd never *see* you again! I was so *lonely* the whole trip!"

"Hey, I promised I'd be here, didn't I?"

She pulled her face back from his neck and looked at him. "Did you? I thought you had abandoned me."

"Never. I'm sure I told you," he said.

"So you did, Mr. Lee." Bob Janos strolled over to the reunion. "I hope your father is well?"

"Well enough to be here," Remo replied. "He's excited. We both are."

"Great, great," Bob replied cheerily, talking around the clinging girl. "I can't want to chat with him some more — we have a big weekend ahead of us!"

Bob's pocket buzzed, and he pulled out his phone.

"You'll have to excuse me...I need to take this," he said. "Glad you made it here, Remo."

"Not as glad as I am," Ewe giggled. Her legs clamped tightly about Remo's waist, and she was grinding herself against his taut stomach.

"Okay, okay," Remo said, taking her wrists and extricating himself from the limb pretzel. "Why don't you get your room, and I'll meet up with you later tonight, okay?"

She pouted. "I thought I'd just stay in your room," she said.

"You don't want that," Remo said. "I've been here on my own for days already without any housekeeping. Towels all over the place, empty beer cans, the trash needs emptying."

"Sounds like my mama's trailer in Mississippi," she said, grinning and biting her lip. "A little trash don't bother me."

"I know, honey," Remo said. "But it bothers me, okay? You'll have a nice, clean room all your own, and we can turn it into our own mess, right? Won't that be fun?"

Ewe hugged herself and squealed. "I'll get signed in!" she said excitedly, trotting to the front desk.

With Ewe temporarily out of the way, Remo focused his hearing on Bob Janos's phone conversation across the dining area. Centering himself, he allowed his hearing to take in the seagull-like susurrus of the crowd, the clinking glassware, even the announcers of the ballgame on the television set playing in the lobby. Then, one at a time, he muted out each sound that was not Bob Janos' voice.

First, the television went silent — one of the tricks he had mastered a long time ago to avoid going crazy having to listen to Chiun's soap operas all the time. Next came the

conversation at the nearest table, where three middle-aged ladies were laughing over glasses of white wine.

The room became more and more devoid of sound, until finally all Remo heard was Bob Janos and the thinner, electronically modified voice of his brother, Tom.

"Yeah," Bob said into the phone. "I made sure everyone knew on the way here that we were going to meet up with another group."

"Good," Tom replied. "I told my group that we would have more allies coming in from across the country to join us. They bought it."

"You going to be okay holed up in there for a while?" Bob asked.

"The channel selection sucks, and the wi-fi is crap," Tom said. "Least you can do is bring up something to eat."

"There's one of those chicken places down the street."

"Don't tease."

Bob laughed. "I'll take care of you, little brother," he said. "I'll be up later to fill you in on everyone on my team, so you can take my place tomorrow."

"Trust me," Tom said. "A day locked away in this room, you'll want to call The Hutch and tell him we need better accommodations next time. It's not like he doesn't have the money."

The desk phone rang, the jangling noise slamming painfully into Remo's eardrum. He winced, and didn't catch what Bob was saying, but the expression on his face indicated that Tom had made him anxious. Whatever Tom said, Bob quickly

disconnected the call right and shoved his phone back into his pants pocket. He took a steadying breath and put his practiced, fake smile back on, stepping forward to work the room again.

Remo went around the corner, stepped through the side doors onto the patio, then followed the sidewalk to a volleyball court, illuminated by a single streetlight. Remo picked up a pebble and flicked it skyward, throwing the area into darkness before taking out his phone to call Smitty.

Smith answered on the first ring. "I hope you have good news," he said.

"I don't know," Remo said. "Any chance a piece of furniture might be important in all this?"

"Remo, I should not have to remind you of the severe nature of what we are facing," Smith said sourly.

"I'm not yanking your chain, Smitty," Remo replied. "I heard one of the Janos boys talking about a 'Hutch.' Sounded like he might have bankrolled the hotel rooms."

Remo could hear keys clicking as Smith entered this new bit of information into the CURE computer. When he returned to the phone, Remo could hear the tension in his voice.

"Hutch Pummel," he said.

"Isn't he the guy who moans and groans about paying less taxes than his butler?" Remo asked.

"He's a billionaire," Smith replied. "He's also an opportunist. From the data I have been able to gather, he has been building a secret organization of high-profile agents, who are working together to steer the opinion of the country

towards increasingly aggressive actions."

"Sounds like our man, all right." Remo felt the itch building up inside him — a chance to dispense his own brand of justice. "Do you know where he is?"

"Colorado," Smith said. "He has an estate west of Denver."

"I can be at the airport in thirty minutes," Remo replied.

"Negative," Smith said. "I need you on the ground in Arlington. The threat against the President is more immediate, and takes priority. Have you made any headway on that?"

"Not yet," Remo said.

"Keep looking," Smith replied. "Call me again in twelve hours with an update."

"I'm not a bodyguard," Remo grumbled, but Smith had already ended the call.

Remo ambled back inside, feeling an uncomfortable anxiousness. CURE had a target. He was the weapon. He was primed to be fired. But he knew Smitty was right. He was needed here first.

Pummel would have to wait.

"There you are!"

Remo looked up to see Mei Hernandez, dolled out in a flowing, sleeveless sundress. Along with the spikes, the blue had been washed out of her hair, which now tumbled down around her shoulders, exuding femininity.

"I've been looking all over for you," she purred, sidling up to him.

"I can be a hard guy to find," Remo said dryly.

"A hard guy is good to find," Mei replied, her eyes twinkling with mischief, her palm rubbing up the inside of Remo's thigh.

"Let's get a drink first," Remo offered, taking her hand and leading her back into the dining area. He poured her a glass of wine and handed it to her. She sipped it and looked up at him seductively. As she did so, he reached over and stroked a nerve on the back side of her neck. Her eyes rolled upward, and the glass tumbled from her hand, spilling alcohol down her cleavage.

"Oh dear," Remo said. "Let's get you upstairs and cleaned up." But as she barely held onto consciousness, the world swimming around her, Mei could not hear Remo's voice. She was vaguely aware that she was walking, that Remo had his arm around her, and that they were going to their room, all of which made her happy and giggly. Anyone watching saw a man and his tipsy date making their way up to a hotel room where they could easily imagine what would happen next.

Upon entering the room, Remo laid Mei on the bed, then ran his thumb gently along the top of her left temple, putting the girl to sleep safely for the rest of the night.

Opening the bedroom window, Remo tapped the sides of the screen, popping it out of its frame so that he could step onto the sill, his head and shoulders outside. The rough brick made for easy purchase, and soon he had scaled the wall all the way up to the roof. This would be a good place to meditate, he thought. Collect himself, push down any urges, center himself.

He looked up at the full moon rising in the east, and had

the strangest sensation that it was laughing at him. He dismissed the notion, and pressed his palms together, elbows out, eyes closed, and directed his focus inward.

He only opened his eyes once, an hour before sunrise, when a sweaty figure with a duffel bag used a key card to let himself into the side entrance.

CHAPTER SIXTEEN

REMO CALLED SMITH as instructed. He had nothing new to report, but Smith still insisted on calls every six hours.

Wandering around the confines of the hotel was giving him cabin fever. During the day, most of the protesters were out and about, walking the streets and seeing the sights, so there was little opportunity to question any of them to see who might be a little too keyed up: rapid heartbeat, excessive sweating, unnecessary blinking, or any other sign that could indicate someone was hiding something. He had to wait for evening, when everyone congregated back for free dinner and booze.

After grueling conversations with six different people, none of whom had any ulterior motives other than either earning a buck or showing the other side who was right, the Janos of the day approached him. Remo knew it was Tom Janos, having slightly less of a tan and a left earlobe that hung just a fraction lower than his brother's.

"Getting to know everybody?" Tom asked cheerfully. Remo let the twin steer him to a corner of the room away from the rest of the herd.

"Can't help it," Remo said. "I'm a people person at heart."

"Nothing wrong with that," Tom said with a forced smile. "I'm just worried about your father. I haven't seen much of him."

"He likes to stay to himself," Remo said. "A good day for him is sitting in front of the television watching a marathon of his favorite soaps."

"Soaps?" Tom asked. "Those things are still on?"

"Well, not here," Remo said. "He can't get them on the television or on my phone. The channel selection sucks and the wi-fi is crap." Remo purposefully parroted Tom Janos's overhead words to him to see if he could rattle the man.

He did.

"Remo, I need you to do me a favor," he said. "A lot of the folks here, you can probably tell they're not really all there. This is a paid vacation for most of them. But we need them, you know? To fill out the crowd, make it look like a real grassroots movement."

"You mean it's not?" Remo asked, feigning sincerity.

Tom Janos smirked. "Come on, Remo," he said. "You're a smart guy, I can tell. You can do better with yourself than carrying a sign and chanting a slogan." He leaned in and whispered. "I've noticed two of the girls here, flighty things, have it pretty bad for you. Why not keep the money, and show them both a good time while everyone else goes to the protest tomorrow? You'd be doing me a big favor, really. Their hearts just aren't into this, and I'm afraid one of them might get hurt, you know? I mean, you remember what happened to that girl in Little Rock."

"Marissa Meyer," Remo said, barely keeping the edge off his voice.

"Right," Tom replied. "I would hate for something like that to happen to either of them. You can take care of them for me though, can't you? A strapping man like yourself?"

Remo allowed himself a crooked smile. "I can take care of them," he said.

Tom winked. "Good man," he said. "I still want to see your dad out there, though."

"You're not afraid something violent will happen to him?"

"Oh no," Tom said. "Are you?"

Remo smiled. "Not a worry in the world," he replied truthfully.

"Good, good," Tom Janos said, clapping Remo on the shoulder. "Tomorrow night is going to be one for the history books."

• • •

Tom Janos was right. Remo did need to take care of Mei and Ewe. There was, of course, the most expedient option, but that hardly seemed fair to either of them. Still, ducking each of them was a bother that he could do without.

Fortunately for Remo, the answer to his problem was self-evident. Rather than avoid them, he decided to get them both into the same room. He would confess to being a cad, and when they found out what had been going on, they would both be so angry with him that neither would want to see him ever again.

It was a good plan. He could see it all working as he made

his way down the hallway, whistling. When he passed the door to Chiun's room, the door opened, and the Master of Sinanju stepped out.

"It will not work," he said calmly.

"What won't work?" Remo asked.

"Whatever cockamamie plan you have concocted in that mush-filled cavity of a skull," Chiun replied. "You always let out a tuneless wailing whistle whenever you think you are being clever. I take it as my duty to warn you when I see you are about to fail at something."

"This isn't like that, Little Father," Remo said. He told him of his plan to let Mei and Ewe meet, get angry, and storm out, as Chiun nodded understandingly at each step of the plan.

"It will not work," he repeated.

"Bulldookie," Remo retorted. "Of course it will. You've just got to rely on letting jealousy and jilted hearts take their natural course."

"Oh," said Chiun. "I did not realize it was such a simple solution. No wonder your simple mind can understand it. Please, allow me to observe this behavior in action, that I may learn from your great and far-reaching wisdom."

"Okay, you just called me both simple and wise in the same breath," Remo said.

Chiun nodded. "One of those was sarcasm," he responded. "I will leave it to you to work out which is which."

Remo grunted, then walked down the hall to Ewe's door. He thumped on it once, and she flung it open, eyes wide with glee. She went to leap on him once more, and he caught her

on the shoulder, keeping her at arm's length. "Whoa there," he said. "I need to talk to you first. Come with me."

He took her hand and led her down the hall to his room, the room where Mei had been staying since the afternoon she walked out of the refrigerator. Again he thumped the door. Mei opened it to greet him, then paused when she saw Ewe.

"Time to come clean," Remo said, entering the room with Ewe in tow.

Mei slowly turned her head toward Ewe. "What do you mean?" she asked, her eyes smoldering dangerously.

"Remo, honey," Ewe purred, looking the Mexican-Chinese girl up and down. "Who's this foreign tramp?"

"Foreign?" Mei growled. "I was born in Los Angeles, you piece of white trash."

"Ladies, please," Remo said. "This is my fault. I've been playing both of you. But I can't do it anymore. It's weighing on my conscience."

"Heh heh heh," Chiun chuckled in the doorway. "Oh, this is very good. Continue, please."

Remo shook his head. "Listen, I know it was wrong —"

A guttural sound was building deep in Mei's throat. Ewe's lips were peeling back, baring her teeth.

"— and I wouldn't blame either of you if you never wanted to see me again. It's on me. I'm just a bad person."

"Bitch!"

"¡*Puta!*"

"He's *my* man!"

"Not if I kill you for him!"

Both women dove for each other at the same time, nails out to strike.

Both missed. They seemed to pass through each other like ghosts, and each tumbled to the floor, arms and legs flailing.

When they stood up, the aged Master of Sinanju stood between them.

"Foolish women," he said with rebuke. "Has the Master asked you to engage in gladiatorial games for his amusement? Has he directed you to damage each other?"

Both women blushed, feeling shame without fully understanding why.

"No," Chiun continued. "He has not. And you dishonor him with your actions. You bring embarrassment upon his house with these jealous antics. This is not a seemly way to behave for courtesans of the Master of Sinanju."

"Chiun, what are you doing?" Remo asked plaintively.

"Taming your concubines," Chiun replied. "Something you are going to have to learn to do for yourself if you are intent on filling your seraglio. Mind you, it will not be in our house. Tell the Emperor you shall require an additional dwelling. I will not be tripping over women's garments in my twilight years, nor shall I put up with constant prattling. Pay attention, so you can do this on your own when I am gone."

"What's a *concubine*?" Ewe asked, wrinkling her nose.

"You are," Mei spat.

"Enough!" Chiun hissed. "Do you wish the Master to exile you and let you fend against the jackals?"

"Master?" Mei asked. "Who's this 'master' person?"

Remo stepped forward. "I've got it from here, Little Father," he said. "I think."

Remo stood between Chiun and the girls, facing them. "Look," he said. "When I met you, both of you, I didn't really like either of you."

Mei's shoulders sank. Ewe's eyes welled up and her lips quivered.

"But that was then," Remo said quickly. "I did some things I really shouldn't have done, and I'm very, very sorry about that. But I can't have the two of you trying to kill each other, okay?"

He took each of them by a hand, rubbing his thumb into their palms in a circular motion. Both of the girls entered a state of immediate calm.

"It would make me really happy if the two of you could get along," he said softly. "Can you do that? Look out for each other? Take care of each other?"

Ewe sniffled. "That would make you happy?"

"Blissful," Remo said.

"But she's…"

"For me," Remo reiterated, a bit more sternly than he intended. Both girls sat up at attention as though they had been scolded by their father. "Okay?"

They both nodded.

"Now, no more fighting, got it?" he said. "You two could be good friends if you'd just get to know each other a little better. Got it?"

Again, they nodded.

"Good." Remo looked to Chiun. The ancient master shrugged dismissively, but he did not give any reproof, which Remo took for approval. "Now I'm going to have to go away soon," he told them. "Maybe even for a long time. There's some bad stuff that may happen soon, and I want the two of you to keep each other safe. That means no protest march for either of you, understand?"

"Yes sir," Mei nodded. Ewe took the other girl's hand and nodded.

"You're leaving us now?" Mei whined, standing. She stepped forward, catlike, pouting, and placed her palms on Remo's chest.

"Not now," Ewe added, joining her, wrapping her willowy arms around Remo's bicep.

"Uh, ladies," Remo stammered. He looked to Chiun, who turned for the door. "A little help here, Chiun?"

"Do not seek to involve me in your bacchanals," Chiun said. "I have matured beyond such things." He closed the door behind him, and Remo could hear him clucking with disappointment as he shuffled down the hall.

Both the girls pressed against him, expressing their desires to keep him with them for just a few more hours.

Remo let them.

• • •

A few hours after midnight, Remo went to the roof once more, leaving Mei and Ewe snuggled against each other in the bed they shared, each of them too spent to fight, and each knowing the other more intimately than they had before.

He breathed in the chilly, pre-dawn air, taking in the sounds around him. There were hardly any towns that truly slept at night any more, and Arlington was certainly not one of them.

He sniffed at the air, and caught the cloying scent of coffee mixed with caramel, and an unhealthy amount of soy. Looking over the edge of the hotel, he saw the same bedraggled, bearded figure from the night before. His heart was racing, which was not surprising given the amount of caffeine that had to have been racing through his system.

"Whatever gets you through the night, I suppose," Remo muttered to himself. He closed his eyes and turned his focus inward, meditating until just before sunup.

CHAPTER SEVENTEEN

THE FOLLLOWING AFTERNOON, HUTCH Pummel stepped out onto his third-floor balcony, and looked with beatific anticipation toward the east. It was two hours later in Arlington. Rush hour would begin in about an hour. He wondered how many people were cognizant enough of local happenings to leave work early, realizing that a protest would further ensnarl the perpetually heavy traffic near Arlington National Cemetery.

He sipped an iced tea, and watched the shadow of his mansion grow longer before him. All the actors were on their marks. The curtain was lifting. The final act was about to be played out.

Hutch Pummel smiled, and turned back inside.

Tomorrow was going to be a brand-new day for America.

• • •

In Arlington, the lobby of the hotel had devolved into the sort of chaos reserved for Black Friday shopping and DMV offices. People were packed shoulder-to-shoulder as they jostled out the double doors to the parking lot, where Bob Janos checked his clipboard, looking up names and directing people to their assigned buses.

There were six buses at the ready; three were in the parking lot, and three were parked on the street around the back of the hotel. As they boarded, protesters were given signs, and allowed to pull on any slogan-bearing shirts they brought with them, having been instructed to conceal any such items until departure, in order to prevent the press from knowing where they were staying before the march.

Each three-bus caravan would take a different route to the memorial site, arriving from opposite directions.

"Tammy Farley," Bob Janos murmured, looking down the list. "Second bus in the back, honey. Next?" A young man with his head shaved stepped forward.

"Tim Keeler," he said.

"Keeler…Keeler…Right. Third bus over there on the lot," Bob directed. "Next?"

Remo leaned against a tree, watching each person step forward and get instructions. His frustration grew. He was looking for an assassin in a haystack.

Nearly two-thirds of the people gave no sign that they were anything other paid help, actors who were simply along for the ride. The remaining third, however, gave off more than enough wonky vibes, and any one of them could be a potential loose cannon. If someone did not get on the bus, Remo would investigate further, but so far, everyone was accounted for.

"Craig Lafferty."

Remo recognized the jittery figure reporting for duty as the fellow who came in during the wee hours of the morning. He could have been out drinking each night, but Remo never

knew someone to stay out chugging soy lattes. He found himself rotating his wrists, absently.

"Lafferty," Janos mumbled, running his pencil down his list. "There you are. First bus, over there on the lot."

Remo watched as Craig Lafferty walked to the bus, and stumbled his way up the steps. He watched him through the darkened windows until he saw him find a seat and sit in it.

"Guess that rules him out," Remo muttered to himself. He continued waiting as the crowd thinned out.

When there were less than a dozen people still waiting to board, Remo stepped up.

"Remo," Bob greeted him. "Ready to roll out?"

"Just about," he said. "I need to go inside and help Chiun with a few things first. Can you tell me what bus we need to get on?"

Bob looked through the list as Remo counted all the unmarked names. "Remo Lee," Bob mused to himself. "Heh. I never met a Remo before, and now we have two on the list."

"I bet we have the same birthday, too," Remo said, grinning lopsidedly.

"Brothers from a different mother, right?" Bob joked. "Your bus is over there," he said, pointing toward the lot. "You're on the back one, and your dad is on the front one. Of course, you can help him on, if you need to."

"Thanks," Remo said. He stepped away and went inside. Counting everyone still checking in, himself and Chiun twice, and Mei and Ewe upstairs, everyone was present and accounted for. Which meant nothing, of course. The potential

killer might just be using the buses as a means of getting closer to the target. Once the shouting matches started, it would be easy to slip away. He would just need to be extra vigilant for anyone who wandered off.

Chiun was waiting for him in the lobby, wearing a gray kimono, upon which was embroidered a dragon in silver thread. When the light caught it just right, the dragon seemed to leap out from the cloth.

"I'm not used to seeing you so monochromatic," Remo said.

"Gray and silver must seem like the same color to your blind eyes," Chiun said. "Nevertheless, they inhabit distinct places on the color palette."

Remo looked down at the white square of folded fabric neatly tucked against Chiun's side. "I'd rather you wear this than that other one you're carrying."

Chiun sniffed. "After all the effort expended in altering it?" he exclaimed. "I would rather march in sackcloth and ashes."

"This is going to be interesting," Remo muttered. "They have a bus waiting for you. You want to take it, or walk?"

Chiun peered at the bus, narrowing his eyes but saying nothing.

They walked.

• • •

Evening shadows fell across Arlington National Cemetery as the first three buses carrying protesters arrived. They emerged wearing t-shirts and carrying signs proclaiming JUSTICE FOR MARISSA, NO COUNTRY FOR OLD

WHITE MEN, and FREE AMERICA FROM HISTORY. The chanting began even before the buses were empty, as the protesters congregated in a cordoned-off area to the north of the Confederate Monument. Their chants competed with the cacophony of the crowd of counter-protesters who had arrived, and who flanked the south side of the monument.

"It's heritage, not hate!" one man shouted.

"Your heritage *is* hate!" another countered.

Neither man recognized the other, despite sharing beers at the same table the night before.

As he surveyed the crowd, Remo realized he would also have to watch the press, and any locals there to watch the circus. Many Arlingtonians found the sport of provoking others too tempting to pass up, and joined with whichever crowd echoed their own latent sentiments.

Remo Williams pulled out the American flag bandana from his pocket, tied it across his forehead, then made his way through the crowd seeking out Bob Janos. The crowd parted easily before him, as a touch here and a brush there deflected the direction of each protester. They did not even know it had happened.

Remo found Bob Janos at the far end of the crowd, a safe distance from the action. It was time to start prying a little harder.

"Is this all we do?" he asked, startling the man.

Bob grinned. "What, shouting slogans and carrying a sign isn't satisfying enough for you?"

"Oh sure, sure," Remo said. "But look at those people."

He indicated the protesters who were demanding the removal of the monument. "Too bad nobody does something about them," he suggested. "I mean, they're here, all in one place. It wouldn't be hard to, you know…" Remo pointed his finger at the crowd and cocked his thumb.

"Why, Mister Lee," Bob replied slyly. "I didn't know you harbored such animosity against your fellow Americans."

"Real Americans love their country, right or wrong," Remo said.

"Hey, love it or leave it, am I right?" Bob Janos grinned, crossed his arms and watched the drama play out. "Keep the faith, Mister Lee," he said. "Maybe some day you'll get your wish."

He turned to where Remo had been just beside him.

Nobody was there.

• • •

Once more Remo cut a clean swathe through the crowd of protesters until he reached the demarcation line. He stepped under the police tape, and strode purposefully into the next group.

"He's attacking us!" a thin man in a hockey mask cried.

"You can't be here!", a slightly chubby woman with a crewcut shrieked. "This is a safe space! No Nazis! No Nazis!"

Those around her joined in on the chanting. "No Nazis! No Nazis!"

Remo put up both hands. "Excuse me, just passing through, really," he said disarmingly. "Porta-johns were all occupied on the other side."

A young girl and an older man wearing a pink knit stocking cap with cat-ears sewn onto it started dancing a circle around him. "No Nazis! No Nazis! No Nazis!"

"Okay," Remo said. "I asked nicely." His arm flashed out faster than anyone could register. Suddenly the older man was flat on his back, and the girl found herself running forward faster than her legs could carry her, causing her to fall face-first into the grass.

Crewcut Lady shouted in outrage. "He hit them! He hit a girl!"

"I'm getting really tired of you," Remo said. "But I don't have time for this." He stepped past her, into the crowd, with only the occasional cry of pain marking his path until he emerged out the other side.

He saw Tom Janos several dozen yards away. *Both the boys are keeping a safe distance from the action*, Remo thought. *What am I not seeing?*

As he approached the other twin, he remembered his bandana, and reached up to unfurl it, obscuring the lower part of his face. "Probably should have done that earlier," he said to himself. "Saved myself some bother."

"You okay, friend?" Tom Janos asked. "Oh, Remo. It's you. Everything okay?"

"Mostly okay," he said, making a show of looking toward the counter-protesters. "Just having some trouble keeping my emotions in check. My grandfather died to stop the Nazis, and now they're on our doorstep. It makes my blood boil, you know? I want to follow in his footsteps and make America

safe from fascist scum like them."

Tom Janos nodded understandingly. "I hear you," Tom said. "But, you know, it's a free country. They have a First Amendment right to speak what little mind they have."

Remo grumbled. "But they shouldn't," he replied.

Tom smiled. "Maybe someday," he said with a wink. "Maybe someday sooner than you think."

"From your lips to God's ears," Remo said.

"Oh, we can do better than God," Tom said. Remo cocked his head and gave him a curious look. "Let's just say that, after tonight, the south is *never* going to rise again."

Remo put his hands in his pockets and ambled back to the perimeter. Once he was inside the throng, he began making his way around it, jostling against people, feeling them for weapons. He still had a potential assassin to find, and time was short.

He made his way through two dozen people when he stopped dead in his tracks. He sniffed the air again, and caught the distinct smell of nitroamine mixed with fresh mulch.

Following the scent took him to the edge of the monument itself, which was protected by a cordon of armed guards to keep away any would-be vandals. Remo took note of the ground around the memorial. It had been carefully tamped down to appear unaltered, but Remo could see lines in the dirt where a shovel had dug in. The scent of C-4 emanated from the disturbed areas.

He pulled the bandana from his face and absently folded it up into a tight triangle before slipping it back into the pocket

of his black chinos, then skirted the perimeter of the protesters and the armed guards.

Without anyone realizing it, he was suddenly on the other side of the guards, stepping carefully closer and closer to the base of the monument. Keeping to the shadows, he began to pace along the foundation, noting the quantities of C-4, and where it had been placed.

Remo looked up toward the top of the monument, taking in its sheer size, and let out a silent whistle. The amount of explosive material laid in here was more than overkill. It would not just take out all the protesters on both sides — it would likely send this chunk of stone flying a good mile through the air.

Remo pulled out his smart phone and dialed Smith.

"Remo," Smith barked curtly. "Have you found a smoking gun?"

"No," Remo said, once more looking the Confederate Memorial up and down. "But I think I just found the bullet."

CHAPTER EIGHTEEN

ALMOST EXACTLY ONE MILE from the protest, the "B'nai B'rith Memorial Dinner for Marissa Meyer" was underway.

Three Secret Service agents guarded every entrance. They were the visible deterrents. The invisible deterrents included at least twice that number of plainclothes agents inside, who mingled with the guests. The buildings on all four sides of the Sheraton Pentagon City had snipers set up on their roofs.

"Bricklayer takes the lectern in five," a voice squawked in all their earpieces, using the code name for the current POTUS. Their eyes scanned for unfriendly faces.

At his place at the table, the President nodded somberly as the Vice-President got into the closing statements of his speech.

Having a great time at the memorial dinner, the President thumbed into the message box on his smart phone. *The Jewish people here love me. Voted big for me too. Will again!*

He thumbed the submit button, and looked up once more as his second-in-command drove home his main selling point — that hatred had no place in the land of the free and the home of the brave. The President set his phone down and clapped softly along with everyone else.

When he picked it back up, a new message box opened.

Projectile attack possible. Leave immediately. S.

The President took a breath, looked nervously toward the room's exit, then toward the roof. "What does he mean, *projectile?*" he said to himself. "A missile? It'd get shot down."

A loud applause made him look up. The Vice-President had just announced him, and was clapping while looking in his direction.

The President waved with one hand and smiled, while his other quickly thumbed in a text reply: *I'm on next. Handle it.*

Standing with a confidence he did not completely believe, the President shook hands with the Vice, and then began to speak.

• • •

At his office in Rye, Smith glowered sourly at the received reply, before tapping the button that digitally scoured any trace of the conversation from both phones and all hops in between. Remo would have to find the killer now, or America would be in mourning within minutes.

• • •

"Of course he's going to stay," Remo said. "Can't you hack into the hotel and set off the fire sprinklers or something to get everyone out of there?"

In fact, Smith had considered that very tactic. "The resulting chaos would put the Secret Service at a disadvantage," he replied. "Just because there is a potential assassin we know does not mean there is not another one that we do not."

"So, I need to find a guy with a detonator, and fast," Remo said. "Fine. What do we know? There's enough C-4 here to launch a giant concrete statue like a rocket. It would have taken days to plant that much." He paused. "No, not days. He'd be

seen. It would have taken nights. Someone working late, every night." Remo's began to scan the mass of protesters again, this time looking — and smelling — for someone very distinct.

"Smitty, I think I know who I'm looking for," he said. "I'll call you back."

Remo slid through the crowd like an eel through seawater, until he caught wind of the familiar scent of soy lattes. He turned just in time to see the jittery guy making his way out of the group and toward the porta-johns. He passed them and continued walking, picking up his pace from a stroll to more of a trot.

"I don't think so, Mister Coffee," Remo growled, setting off after him.

• • •

Craig Lafferty was sweating through his hoodie. His stomach gurgled from the 'yumbo' latte he had chugged before getting on the bus, his second of the day. He briefly regretted not stopping to use one of the porta-johns, but he was too excited.

His hands trembled. Reaching into his pocket, his fingers felt the remote detonator switch, but instead chose to grab a well-worn fidget spinner that sat beside it. Craig found spinning the little toy calming. It gave his fingers something to do as he counted down the minutes until he changed the world.

"Cool toy."

He gasped and turned, dropping the triple-bladed toy to the ground. The thin man who had startled him wore a tight black t-shirt, tucked into equally black chinos.

"Sorry," he said. "Didn't mean to make you drop it." He

bent over to pick it up, and Craig noticed the man's wrist was unusually thick. He held it up between his thumb and forefinger and glanced at it. "What do you do with this?" the man asked.

"You, uh, you just spin it," Lafferty stammered. He looked back toward the crowd in the distance, then checked his watch. The stranger flicked one of the blades with his finger, and it began to spin.

The man nodded. "Pretty cool," he said. "That all it does?"

"Ah, yeah," Lafferty said. "It just…yeah, that's it." He thought everyone knew what a fidget spinner was, and felt awkward having to explain its purpose.

The man flicked it again while it spun, making it go even faster. Craig Lafferty could hear the blades making a whizzing noise as they went around.

"You've really got that thing going," Lafferty said. "Probably won't stop for a good ten minutes. That'd be a record." Stranger or no stranger, he was on a deadline. He began to casually slip his hand into the pocket with the detonator.

"Oh, I don't thin it'll spin that long," the man said. He gave it one more flick, and suddenly the toy was no longer between his thumb and finger.

Craig Lafferty instinctively looked to the ground for the toy, but it was too dark. Then it was too red. Then it was dark *and* red. He felt as though he were falling to the ground — then through the ground.

The impact of his face against the dirt drove the fidget spinner deeper into the ridge of his nose, where it had neatly embedded itself, ending the consciousness, and then the life, of Craig Lafferty.

Remo Williams gingerly inspected the man's pocket and took out the remote detonator. He squeezed it gently, and the sides bowed out until the casing popped open. He pinched off the wire that connected to the relay, rendering the device useless.

He called Smitty to give him the good news.

• • •

Bob Janos was concerned. It was three minutes past the big moment, and so far there had been no earth-shattering kaboom. He briefly wondered if the plan had gone off track, but put that worry aside. The boss would have a backup plan in place. He was a smart guy.

"Something bothering you, Bob?"

Bob turned with a start. "Remo!" he said. "Man, you walk on cat's feet, you know that?"

Remo looked at him grimly. "Get to the Memorial Amphitheater," he said tersely. "Ten minutes."

"What? Why? What are you talking about?" Bob asked.

"You know," Remo said. "So does 'The Hutch.'"

The blood drained from Bob Janos's face. He knew something was off about this Remo Lee character the whole time, but he never considered he might have been a plant from the boss to check up on them. He opened his mouth to make some excuse for why things had not gone as planned. He would pin the blame on unreliable agents, or even his brother Tom if he had to.

But Remo had already disappeared into the darkness.

• • •

Across the venue, Tom Janos was having similar worries. He

jumped as he felt the touch of a hand on his shoulder.

"Goddammit, man," he said, recognizing Remo. "Make some noise, will you?" He gave a nervous laugh to gather his composure.

Remo pointed across the cemetery to the Memorial Amphitheater. "You're needed over there," he said. "It's for 'The Hutch.'" Remo heard Tom Janos's heart quicken, and smiled grimly to himself. These men were deathly afraid of their boss, confirming Remo's hunch about the man who was pulling all the strings. He backed away into the shadows before Tom realized he had gone, and watched as Tom made a beeline for the covered enclosure.

• • •

Bob and Tom Janos arrived at the amphitheater almost simultaneously.

"What the hell's going on?" Tom hissed.

"How should I know?" Bob replied. "The key guy was in your camp. Did you lose him?"

"No way," Tom said. "I had eyes on him the whole time, right up until the moment he went to set it off."

"Well, what happened to him?" Bob asked.

"He died."

Both men turned toward the direction of the voice, which came from a dark corner of the amphitheater. They could barely make out the silhouette of a slender man in the blackness. The darkened figure held his hand out into a pool of light, filtering into the area from a street light. From that hand unfurled a bandana.

The red, white, and blue of the American flag glowed

vibrantly in the lamplight.

"Remo?" both men said together, then looked at each other, realization dawning on them at the same time.

"This means something," Remo said, somberly. "It's a symbol that reminds us of who we are. What we've endured. Where we've come from." He stayed in the shadows, letting the tiny flag remain the visual focus of the twins. "It's not something that covers your actions. It's not something you hide behind. It stands for unity — the United States of America."

Remo Williams stepped into the light.

"And so do I."

In two strides he was on the twins, his arms wide. Faster than they could react, he knocked their heads together. He continued applying pressure, grinding their heads into each other, until there was only one head between them — half Bob, half Tom, a grotesque scar of blood bisecting the near-symmetry of the merged face.

Remo exhaled. *This felt right*, he thought. *This was what he was meant for.*

Remo smiled grimly.

He still had more to do.

• • •

As he made his way back to the Confederate Memorial, Remo noted the shouting had died down to nearly nothing. There was still one distinct voice, however, screeching in a high pitch.

"Oh no," Remo groaned. "Chiun, what are you doing?"

When Remo got to the scene, both crowds were looking up to the top of the monument, as were all the news cameras. Even

the guards looked upward, some scratching their heads in confusion.

Following their gaze, Remo saw Chiun standing atop the dome, next to the carved female figure of 'The South.' He wore the white KKK robe he had been given, but the garment had been reworked with black beads, patterned into tiger stripes from shoulder to hem. The matching hood had likewise been altered, and it now bore an uncanny resemblance to a dunce cap, a thought Remo promised himself never to disclose to Chiun.

"Why do you all march and scream impotently into the night?" Chiun shouted from his perch. "What do your mere words accomplish when your hands are more effective?"

Remo shook his head. He had just saved the monument from certain destruction, and now Chiun was trying to motivate the crowd into tearing it down by hand.

"Does your past offend you?" he cried. "Then pluck it out. That will make it unhappen, no? Reach out and take this symbol with your hands, crush it, and absolve yourselves of all guilt!"

The crowd began to murmur on both sides. "Is he for real?" "Crazy old man."

"Come!" Chiun exhorted them. "Come, and change your history!"

"History doesn't change," someone called out from the crowd.

Chiun smiled. "Then change your future," he said. "Does this rock I stand upon inspire you with pride? Does it fill you with shame? It is merely a carved rock. It means nothing other than that dead men are buried here. Honor or dishonor their

memories as you wish, for they are not my ancestors. But know that they laugh at you from the void for your foolishness."

Remo noticed the crowd dissipating on both sides. Signs were tossed to the ground as a few people, then a few dozen more, turned to leave, slump-shouldered and shamed.

"He's trying to shut us down!" cried one of the few protesters who remained. She tried to rouse the others into joining her, chanting: "No Nazis! No Nazis!"

Chiun cackled and joined her until she shut up in embarrassment. "You need monsters to validate you?" Chiun called out. "All of you have become the monsters you claim to fear," he intoned, looking out over both groups. "Look inside yourselves, and you will see that I speak the truth."

By now neither group could be called a crowd. There were only a handful of people left on either side, as more and more people walked away.

Remo knew those who remained were too deeply invested in their beliefs to give up. They needed to feel hate in order to define their existence. But Chiun had held up a mirror to the rest of them, and shown them something that they would always remember.

"Come down, Little Father," Remo called. "Sorry about this, guys," he told the guard beside him. "He gets a little nutty without his meds."

"I do not take 'meds,'" Chiun scoffed, suddenly standing beside Remo and startling the guard.

"I know you don't," Remo said, patting his shoulder and winking at the guard. "I know. Let's just get out of here."

CHAPTER NINETEEN

"WHY DO YOU RUSH ABOUT like a head without a chicken?"

Remo was quickly but carefully packing Chiun's belongings. "No need to hang around here longer than we have to," he said. "Upstairs has more work for me, and I'd like to get right on it."

Chiun frowned. "You have been most eager to exercise your skills lately. It is unlike you."

Remo paused. He had not sat down with Chiun to talk about the urges he felt, and he realized this was the opportunity he had been looking for.

After having removed the Janos twins, he had felt a combined sense of calm and urgency. He was satisfied, yet still hungry. And he liked it.

Maybe he did not have to tell Chiun right away.

"I admit, I began to harbor some small worries about you," Chiun continued. "But if you are performing in the service of the Emperor Smith, that means more gold for the children of Sinanju. How can I disapprove of such a thing?"

"Right," Remo said. "Exactly. And the sooner we can earn that gold, the better, right?"

There was, of course, another reason Remo was in a hurry to leave Arlington behind. In fact, there were two of them, just

a few doors down the hall. With luck, Remo would already be on his way back to Rye before Mei and Ewe woke up.

That hope evaporated the moment Remo opened the door to leave, finding the two girls standing there, Ewe's fist raised in preparation to knock at the door.

"Oh!" she said. "You are back after all."

Remo groaned inwardly. "Hello, girls," he said. "Have you been out here the whole time?"

"We watched for you out the window," Mei said. She tucked her chin down, demurely, prepared for a scolding.

"We saw you come in," Ewe added meekly. "We waited as long as we could, but…we missed you." Ewe was back in denim shorts and her sleeveless white blouse that accentuated her willowy arms. She looked at the trunks, stacked and ready to go. "Are we leaving now?"

"Are we…what?" Remo sputtered Chiun chuckled, and Remo cut his eyes at him. "No, *we* are not leaving now. I mean, yes, we *are* all leaving, just…not together."

Both girls tilted their heads, confused.

He sighed. "Look, I travel a lot for my job," he said.

"I love to travel," Mei said enthusiastically.

"I've always wanted to," added Ewe.

"No," Remo said. "Girls, look…don't you have homes to go to? Lives to get back to living?"

"So?" said Mei.

"No," said Ewe.

"Heh heh heh," Chiun snickered.

"Not helping," Remo muttered under his breath.

"Not trying," Chiun replied with amusement.

Remo tried a more direct approach. "Okay, you. I mean, Ewe," he said. "Where did you live before you signed up for the march?"

"With my Mama in her trailer," she said.

"Good!" he said. "You have a place to go. I want you to go there."

Ewe began to sniffle. "But I don't want to go there," she said. "Please don't make me. Everyone there is mean to everybody. They call people names, and I can't have any black friends, and the men just want to get drunk and rough with me." A tear streaked down her cheek. "I used to be fine with it, but now..."

"Do not be swayed by her tears, Remo," Chiun said. "Send her back."

Remo shook his head and looked to Mei. "You. Not Ewe, Mei," he said. "You have a business. You repair refrigerators."

Mei nodded. "I'd give it all up to be with you," she said.

"I don't want you to give it up," Remo said. "In fact, I need you to expand your business."

"Expand?"

Remo put his hands on Ewe's shoulders and turned her to face Mei. "Yes," he said. "Meet your newest employee. Ewe, what can you do?"

Ewe stuttered. "I can...make coffee? And wash clothes?"

"See?" Remo said. "She had to learn those things. She can learn refrigerator repair, too."

"You want me to teach her...?" Mei asked, her voice trailing off.

Remo cupped her chin and her body sagged. She stared up

at him with unadulterated adoration.

"I want you to take her in," Remo said. "Make her your apprentice. Teach her everything you know — and take care of her, okay?"

"Of course, Remo," Mei said dreamily.

"And you," Remo said, putting his palm on Ewe's neck. She trembled and purred as she looked up into his face, expressing pure longing. "Go with Mei. Listen to her. Help her with all that cooking and coffee-making and laundry-doing. And take care of her, right?"

"Anything for you, Remo," she replied.

"Good," Remo said. "Great. I'm glad we've got this all worked out. Now, go back to your rooms and pack, and go straight to Mei's place." He kissed both of them on the cheek, punctuation to his instructions. Both girls giggled, and ran out of the room, each stealing a glance back at the Master of Sinanju — their master.

"You are just going to leave them to their own devices?" Chiun asked.

"There's no room in this business for Ewe and Mei," Remo said. "Just you and me."

Chiun shook his head ruefully. "You speak in riddles," he complained.

"I learned from the best, Little Father," said Remo, putting his hand on the bony shoulder of the ancient master. "Come on, let's get out of here before they come back. Smitty has one more thing for me to clean up."

CHAPTER TWENTY

IN HIS COUNTRY MANSION in Colorado, Hutch Pummel was in an uncharacteristically poor mood. He was not so naïve as to believe setbacks could not happen — during his long life, he had suffered many.

"But this was such an absolute cock-up," he fumed. He paced back and forth at the head of the ridiculously long table. Cheryl Sparks kept silent, afraid to be noticed, lest she become a target of Pummel's wrath. Kirk Ehrlichman sat at attention, having rushed to the mansion first, not daring to risk being absent.

"This would never have happened if I'd —" Hal Bluntman was cut off quickly by a hard glance from Pummel. Then his gaze softened.

"No," he said. "This is none of your fault. This was the Janos brothers' play. And when I see those failures again — and believe me, I will — I am going to…"

"I believe you."

Everyone turned to face the entrance of the great meeting room. The doors were closed, though nobody had heard them shut.

A man stood in front of them. He was of a slender build, with deep-set eyes, and he wore a tight black t-shirt and matching chinos.

"Who the devil are you?" Pummel asked. "Never mind. It doesn't matter." He walked to an electronic box at the head of the table and pressed a button. "Henry? We have an intruder." He waited a second, then pressed it again. "Henry?"

"Henry couldn't make it," the man said, walking up the side of the room. "But I'm here. I'm Remo, by the way. And you've been a very bad boy."

Hutch Pummel drew himself up to his full stature. "I have no idea what you're talking about."

Remo grinned. "Sure you do," he said. "And I'm not even talking about your little over-the-top assassination plot you staged in Arlington. Nice plan, by the way. No evidence of it being anything more than a freak accident. As a pro, I've got to tip my hat to you. It really was inspired." He paused for a moment before he continued. "No, I'm here about all of it." He swept his arms out, indicating the room in general. "The whole long game — overthrowing the United States. That's not something I can allow."

"Oh, really," Pummel said with a forced laugh. "And just what makes you think I want to overthrow the government? I'm a respected businessman. I'm a billionaire, for Christ's sake. Why would I want to give up all my power to lead this pitiful country?"

The man in black shook his head. "'Pitiful?' See, that just tells me you don't get it," Remo said. "It's not pitiful. It's beautiful. Everyone can do just about anything they want. We have freedoms. We have rights."

Kirk Ehrlichman snorted derisively. "Rights!" he said.

Remo looked down at Ehrlichman. "Yeah," he said.

"Rights. For instance, I have the right to swing my fist…"

"I know that old canard," Ehrlichman said. "You have the right to swing your fist, but that right ends at the tip of my —"

Kirk Ehrlichman cried out in pain as Remo's fist crunched into the middle of his face, his nostrils exploding with blood. Contessa Schilling screeched as the spray graffitied a crimson pattern across her six hundred dollar blouse.

"Hey!" Ehrlichman cried out. "You can'd do dad!"

"You see," Remo addressed the rest of the room. "I'm the exception that *protects* the rule."

Pummel gave Remo an appraising look. "What agency are you with, son?" he asked. "Whatever they're paying you, I can triple it. A man with your skills could go far."

"I don't work for anyone you've heard of," Remo said.

"So, not FBI?" Pummel asked, grinning. "Not law enforcement of any kind? My friend, you've made so many mistakes I don't have time to even list them all. You've violated our due process. You wouldn't dare go to news agencies, or you'd expose yourself, and your agency." He walked straight up to Remo until the two men stood inches apart. "Just exactly what *was* the plan here, Remo?" he asked. "You have all this so-called information on us, and nothing you can do with it. So tell me, Remo. Tell me what happens next."

Remo returned a grim smile. His dead eyes glinted under his brow.

"I do."

• • •

Fifteen minutes later, Remo sat on the side of a green hill, watching the smoke curl skyward from the collapsing remains

ALFAGUARA

ALFAGUARA JUVENIL

www.leeresunbuenplan.es

ALFAGUARA

www.leeresunbuenplan.es

© De esta edición:
   2008, Santillana Infantil y Juvenil, S. L.
   1997, Grupo Santillana de Ediciones, S. A.
   Avenida de los Artesanos, 6. 28760 Tres Cantos (Madrid)
   Teléfono: 91 744 90 60

ISBN: 978-84-204-6501-2
Depósito legal: M-50.600-2008
Printed in Spain - Impreso en España

Primera edición: septiembre 1997
Vigésimo segunda edición: marzo 2014

Diseño de la colección:
MANUEL ESTRADA

Ilustraciones:
JUAN RAMÓN ALONSO

Selección y prólogo:
ANA PELEGRÍN

SANTILLANA

Poesía española para jóvenes

Selección y prólogo de Ana Pelegrín

Ilustraciones de Juan Ramón Alonso

ALFAGUARA

Prólogo

En los libros de misterio, en las películas de aventuras, el joven héroe suele llegar en su búsqueda ante un muro cerrado a cal y canto, frente a una cueva igualmente sellada en la que se guardan tesoros fabulosos...

Pero el joven héroe sabe que existe un pasaje secreto que deberá descubrir con su imaginación, su iniciativa, su capacidad para sortear obstáculos hasta encontrar la clave.

Así es este libro de poemas, como un pasaje secreto que se abre cuando te propongas leerlo con gesto decidido e imaginativo, aguzando el oído y la sensibilidad para atrapar las voces e imágenes que encierran las palabras.

Este libro de poemas tiene entradas diferentes. Por ejemplo, si quieres planear un viaje, traza libremente la recta de pueblos, aldeas y ciudades de la geografía guiado por las palabras (capítulo IV: «Coplas de toda España»: «Rutas»; «Ávila, Málaga, Cáceres»; «Límites convencionales»; «Lo traigo andado»).

También existen unas contadas rutas fluviales: «El niño miraba el agua», «Arroyuelo sin nombre»...

España, siempre en el corazón de los poetas, a veces es una dolorosa herida en el ausente y más aún en el desgarro del exilio («Cancioncillas de ausencias»); pero también alienta un hondo anhelo por mantener alerta la esperanza de la paz («En el nombre de España, paz»).

Hay dos puertas (capítulos II y III) en este libro que tienen igual color porque nacen de un mismo coloreado corazón: el amor a la naturaleza, a los pájaros, los bichos, los animales, los árboles, el cielo, el sol y la luna, el invierno y el verano. Un sentimiento que se transparenta en la mirada atenta y emocionada a todo lo que se mueve y sucede cada día («Calle del arrabal», «Sol de invierno», «Canción primaveral»). Una manera de mirar y escuchar con el corazón hasta el más pequeño de los sucesos: los

pájaros que no están pero que cantan en el poema, una lagartija escapando en un muro, una flor que se abre como un relámpago de luz (Abrió la flor del cardón / y todo se iluminó). Esa manera de ver lo que no se ve, de sentir, de emocionarse con las palabras es como tener en el corazón otro corazón ardiente para aprender a amar y enamorarse de la vida.

La espontaneidad del niño y el joven mantiene, en esa mirada creativa, una capacidad para transformar parecida a la imagen poética que ve la luna «como un pájaro de fuego».

Los poemas esperan ser descubiertos a viva voz por una lectura imaginativa y sensible. La misma voz que impulsa tu propia creación poética para estar más cerca de los grandes poetas de la cultura española: Juan Ramón Jiménez, Lorca, Alberti, Cernuda, Lope de Vega, Del Valle, Ferrán, Hierro…, haciéndote compartir una emoción que no te dejará olvidarlos.

Pero también la poesía española nos regala otra sorpresa: es la recreación colectiva de poemas que han rodado por la imaginación de muchas generaciones y aún están vivos en la memoria. Son los romances: algunos fijados en la escritura como el del infante Arnaldos, el que navega por el tiempo en su mágica barca; otros se han repetido oralmente a través de siglos y tienen variantes, como es fácil comprobar en las versiones de «Doncella guerrera».

Todos los romances de tradición oral moderna que cuentan antiguas historias los he recogido personalmente por toda España y los dejo en tus manos, como un arca que guarda un fabuloso tesoro, un legado de palabras y de experiencia poética, para que leas y te apropies de ellos, porque tuyos son, te pertenecen.

Y ahora, abras por donde abras el libro te introducirás, con imaginación, mirada y corazón, en el escenario poético… Comienza la aventura.

ANA PELEGRÍN

I

NIÑOS, DONCELLAS, CABALLERITOS

Anónimo

TERESILLA HERMANA, HERMANO PERICO

Teresilla hermaná
de la farira rirá,
hermana Teresá.

Periquillo hermanó,
de la fariri runó,
hermano Pericó.

ANÓNIMO

SOL, SOL…

Sol, sol, gigi, A B C,
enamoradico vengo
de la sol fa mi re.

Iba a ver a mi madre
a quien mucho amé;
íbame cantando
lo que os diré.

Sol, sol, gigi, A B C,
enamoradico vengo
de la sol fa mi re.

Anónimo

CANCIONCILLA DEL DONAIRE

No tengo cabellos, madre,
mas tengo bonico donaire.

No tengo cabellos, madre,
que me lleguen a la cinta;
mas tengo bonico donaire
con que mato a quien me mira.
Mato a quien me mira, madre,
con mi bonico donaire.

No tengo cabellos, madre,
mas tengo bonico donaire.

GIL VICENTE

CANTIGA

Muy graciosa es la doncella,
¡cómo es bella y hermosa!

Digas tú, el marinero
que en las naves vivías;
si la nave o la vela o la estrella
es tan bella.

Digas tú, el caballero
que las armas vestías,
si el caballo o las armas o la guerra
es tan bella.

Digas tú, el pastorcico
que el ganadico guardas,
si el ganado o los valles o la sierra
es tan bella.

ANÓNIMO

TRES MORILLAS ME ENAMORAN

Tres morillas me enamoran
en Jaén:
Axa y Fátima y Marién.

Tres morillas tan garridas
iban a coger olivas,
y hallábanlas cogidas
en Jaén,
Axa y Fátima y Marién.

Y hallábanlas cogidas,
y tornaban desmaídas
y las colores perdidas
en Jaén,
Axa y Fátima y Marién.

Tres moricas tan lozanas,
tres moricas tan lozanas,
iban a coger manzanas
a Jaén,
Axa y Fátima y Marién.

GIL VICENTE

GENTIL SERRANA

¿Por dó pasaré la sierra,
gentil serrana morena?

Tu ru ru ru lá, ¿quién la pasará?
Tu ru ru ru rú, no la pases tú.
Tu ru ru ru ré, yo la pasaré.

Di, serrana, por tu fe:
si naciste en esta tierra,
¿por dó pasaré la sierra,
gentil serrana morena?

Ti ri ri ri rí, queda tú aquí.
Tu ru ru ru rú, ¿qué me quieres tú?
To ro ro ro ró, yo sola estó.

Serrana, no puedo, no,
que otro amor me da guerra.
¿Cómó pasaré la sierra,
gentil serrana morena?

Anónimo

MORENICA ME ERA

(Del cancionero judío sefardí)

Morenica a mí me llaman,
yo blanca nací,
el sol del verano
me hizo a mí ansí.

Morenica graciosica sós.
Morenica y graciosica y *mavra matiamer*[1].

---

[1] *mavra matiamer:* los ojos negros.

Lope de Vega

CABALLERO DE PANAMÁ

—¿De dó viene el caballero?
—Viene de Panamá,
trencelín[1] en el sombrero.
—Viene de Panamá,
cadenita de oro al cuello.
—Viene de Panamá,
con banda[2] y con greguiesco[3].
—Viene de Panamá,
las ligas con rapacejos[4].
—Viene de Panamá,
zapatos al uso nuevo.
—Viene de Panamá.
—¿De dó viene, de dó viene?
—Viene de Panamá.

---

[1] trencelín: trencilla, cinta.
[2] banda: cinta ancha que cruza el pecho.
[3] greguiesco: calzones-pantalones hasta la rodilla.
[4] ligas con rapacejos: ligas con adornos de cintas.

—¿De dó viene el hijodalgo[5]?
—Viene de Panamá,
corto cuello y puños largo.
—Viene de Panamá,
la daga en banda, colgando.
—Viene de Panamá,
guante de ámbar adobado[6].
—Viene de Panamá,
gran jugador del vocablo.
—Viene de Panamá,
enfadoso[7] y mal criado.
—Viene de Panamá,
es amor, llámase Indiano.
—Viene de Panamá,
es chapetón[8] castellano.
—Viene de Panamá,
en criollo disfrazado.
—Viene de Panamá.
—¿De dó viene el caballero?
—Viene de Panamá.

---

[5] hijodalgo: hidalgo, persona de la nobleza.
[6] guante de ámbar adobado: guante bordado con pedrería.
[7] enfadoso: que se enfada con rapidez.
[8] chapetón: en América se decía del europeo recién llegado.

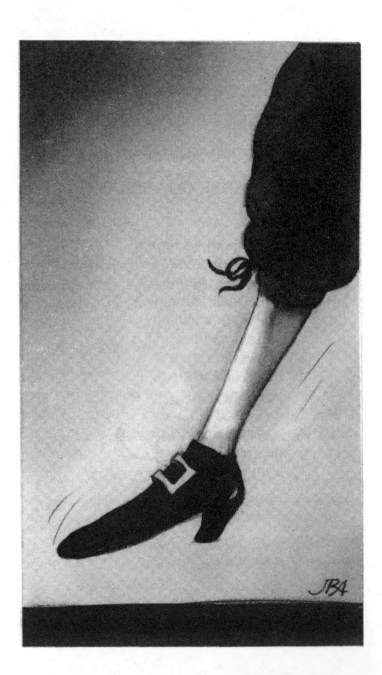

JULIO ALFREDO EGEA

NANA DEL GITANILLO

Me pesa en brazos
la carne morena
de tu cuerpecito.
¡Duérmete, mi amor!
Por el río adelante
va la luna llena
y azota con junco
lobos de carbón.
¡Que no! ¡Que aquí no…!

Ya vuelan los pájaros
negros de tus ojos
a mi corazón.

La fragua distante
levanta en el viento
su constelación.
Yunques y martillos
harán con tus sueños
ánforas de sol.

La rueda del carro,
con polvo de luna,
cesa en su canción.
El caballo esconde
su trote mejor.

¡No llores, mi niño!
¡Duérmete, mi amor!

Miguel de Unamuno

LA MEDIA LUNA ES UNA CUNA...

La media luna es una cuna,
¿y quién la briza?
y el niño de la media luna,
¿qué sueños riza?
La media luna es una cuna,
¿y quién la mece?
y el niño de la media luna,
¿para quién crece?
La media luna es una cuna,
va a luna nueva;
y al niño de la media luna,
¿quién me lo lleva?

Gerardo Diego

SAN BAUDELIO DE BERLANGA

—Que no. —Sí; madre, que sí.
Que yo los vi.

Cuatro elefantes
a la sombra de una palma;
los elefantes, gigantes.
—¿Y la palma? —Pequeñita.
—¿Y qué más?
¿Un quiosco de malaquita?
—Y una ermita.

—Una patraña
tu ermita y tus elefantes.
Ya sería una cabaña
con ovejas trashumantes.
—No. Más bien una mezquita
tan chiquita:
La palma
me llevó el alma.
—Fue solo un sueño, hijo mío.
—Que no, que estaban allí,
yo los vi,
los elefantes.
Ya no están y estaban antes.

(Y se los llevó un judío,
perfil de·maravedí).

JORGE GUILLÉN

SOLEDADES

La Lola...

La niña
se va muy lejos,
Anita,
por el aire, sobre la ola
se va a su puerto.

La niña,
lejos, muy lejos,
con su gracia tan chica,
y Europa
se queda,
       se me queda
          sola.

Luis Cernuda

MÁLIBU

Málibu,
olas con lluvia,
aire de música.

Málibu,
agua cautiva,
gruta marina.

Málibu,
nombre de hada,
fuerza encantada.

Málibu,
viento que ulula,
bosque de brujas.

Málibu,
una palabra,
y en ella, magia.

JORGE GUILLÉN

MANERA ACTUAL DE SER NIÑO

Antonio viaja que viaja
por tierra, por mar, por aire,
va de un continente a otro
porque el mundo ya no es grande,
mira desde su avión
cordilleras y ciudades
como si, soñando aún,
sobre algún mapa trazase
con el dedo rutas, rumbos.
¿Ser hombre es estar de viaje?

MARÍA ELVIRA LACACI

SOLO SÉ...

Solo sé andar muy despacio,
a pie o en bicicleta.
¡Quisiera ser un atleta!
Ave humana del espacio.

Que mi cuerpo en las anillas
fuese flexible y erecto.
Tensos mis músculos. Recto.
Sin encoger las rodillas.

Y ganar muchas medallas
—más que un bravo militar—.
Quisiera también saltar
¡con la pértiga altas vallas!

JAIME FERRÁN

CICLISTAS

Bicicletas de una,
de dos
        y de tres ruedas

se cruzan,
            se entrecruzan;
mecánicas y tercas.

Los hombres que las montan,
ágiles pedalean,

giran enloquecidos,
suben las escaleras.

Y todo,
      todo,
           todo,
en bicicleta.

Una palmada
           y súbitas
al unísono frenan.

Y en su sitio se quedan
inmóviles y quietas.

Otra palmada.

               Arrancan
de nuevo
           y serpentean

por la pista.
              Sin manos
los ciclistas las llevan.

Otra
      y corren de espaldas
entre bromas y veras,

y parece que chocan,
pero no,
           se sortean.

Y parece que caen,
pero no,
           se enderezan.

Y todo, todo, todo.
Y todo, todo, todo,
en bicicleta.

GERARDO DIEGO

BALÓN

Tener un balón, Dios mío.
Qué planeta de fortuna.
Vamos a los Arenales:
cinco hectáreas de desierto,
cuadro y recuadro del puerto.

Qué olor la Tabacalera.
—Suelta ya el balón. Incera.
—No somos once. —No importa.
Si no hay eleven hay seven.
Qué elegante es el inglés:
decir sportman, team, back;
gritar goal, córner, penalty.
(Aún no se ha abierto el Royalty).

—Marca tú la portería:
textos y guardarropía.
—Somos siete contra siete.
Un portero y un defensa,
dos medios, tres delanteros;
eso se llama la uve.
Y a jugar. Vale la carga.
Pero no la zancadilla.
Yo miedo nunca lo tuve.
(Una brecha en la espinilla).

Ya se desinfla el balón.
Sopla tú fuerte la goma.
Ata ya el cuero marrón.
El de badana en colores
déjase a los menores
para botar con la mano.

—Mañana a la Magdalena
a jugar contra el «Piquío».
Y al «Plazuela», desafío.

Tener un balón, Dios mío.

II

ESOS DÍAS AZULES

ANTONIO MACHADO

SOL DE INVIERNO

Es mediodía. Un parque.
Invierno. Blancas sendas;
simétricos montículos
y ramas esqueléticas.

Bajo el invernadero,
naranjos en maceta,
y en su tonel, pintado
de verde, la palmera.

Un viejecillo dice
para su capa vieja:
«¡El sol, esta hermosura
de sol…». Los niños juegan.

El agua de la fuente
resbala, corre y sueña
lamiendo, casi muda,
la verdinosa piedra.

JOSÉ HIERRO

CABALLERO DE OTOÑO

Viene, se sienta entre nosotros,
y nadie sabe quién será,
ni por qué cuando dice *nubes*
nos llenamos de eternidad.

Nos habla con palabras graves
y se desprenden al hablar
de su cabeza secas hojas
que en el viento vienen y van.

Jugamos con su barba fría.
Nos deja frutos. Torna a andar
con pasos lentos y seguros
como si no tuviera edad.

Él se despide. ¡Adiós! Nosotros
sentimos ganas de llorar.

FEDERICO GARCÍA LORCA

PAISAJE

La tarde equivocada
se vistió de frío.

Detrás de los cristales
turbios, todos los niños
ven convertirse en pájaros
un árbol amarillo.

La tarde está tendida
a lo largo del río,
y un rubor de manzana
tiembla en los tejadillos.

JUAN RAMÓN JIMÉNEZ

FIN DE INVIERNO

Cantan, cantan.
¿Dónde cantan los pájaros que cantan?
Llueve y llueve. Aún las casas
están sin ramas verdes. Cantan y cantan
los pájaros. ¿En dónde cantan
los pájaros que cantan?

No tengo pájaros en jaula.
No hay niños que los vendan. Cantan.
El valle está muy lejos. Nada…

Nada. Yo no sé dónde cantan
los pájaros (y cantan, cantan)
los pájaros que cantan.

Anónimo

EN ESTA PLAZUELITA...

En esta plazuelita,
en este llano,
se mantiene la nieve
todo el verano.
¡Cómo llueve!

¡Qué serenita cae la nieve!
Y el aire cierzo
la detiene.

Federico García Lorca

CANCIÓN PRIMAVERAL

Salen los niños alegres
de la escuela,
poniendo en el aire tibio
del abril canciones tiernas.
¡Qué alegría tiene el hondo
silencio de la calleja!
Un silencio hecho pedazos
por risas de plata nueva.

Valle-Inclán

MILAGRO DE LA MAÑANA

Tañía una campana
en el azul cristal
de la paz aldeana.

Oración campesina
que temblaba en la azul
santidad matutina.

Y en el viejo camino
cantaba un ruiseñor,
y era de luz su trino.

La campana de aldea
le dice con su voz
al pájaro que crea.

La campana aldeana
en la gloria del sol
era el alma cristiana.

Al tocar esparcía
aromas del rosal
de la Virgen María.

DÁMASO ALONSO

CALLE DEL ARRABAL

Se me quedó en lo hondo
una visión tan clara,
que tengo que entornar los ojos cuando
pretendo recordarla.

A un lado, hay un calvero de solares;
al otro, están las casas alineadas
porque esperan que de un momento a otro
la Primavera pasará.

                    Las sábanas,
aún goteantes, penden
de todas las ventanas.

El viento juega con el sol en ellas,
y ellas ríen del juego y de la gracia.

Y hay las niñas bonitas
que se peinan al aire libre.

                          Cantan
los chicos de una escuela la lección.
Las once dan.

                Por el arroyo pasa
un viejo cojitranco
que empuja su carrito de naranjas.

ÁNGELA FIGUERA AYMERICH

SIESTA

Entre un álamo y un pino
mi hamaca se balancea.
Hojitas de verde plata
bailan sobre mi cabeza;
hojitas de verde oscuro
el verde las contonea.

Dulce pereza me llueve
del sol que las atraviesa.
Los juncos de celuloide
montan su guardia en la arena.

El Duero moja las cañas
y se abanica con ellas.
El río pasa y se va:
mi barca se queda en tierra.

Llenos de verdes y azules,
mis ojos
se cierran.

Valle-Inclán

ROSA VESPERTINA

Anochece. En la aldea,
un gallo cacarea
mirando el amapol
del sol.

Vacas y recentales
pacen en los herbales,
y canta una mocina
albina.

El reflejo de grana
de la niña aldeana,
enciende al cristalino
lino.

En el fondo del prado,
el heno gavillado,
entre llovizna y bruma
perfuma.

Por la verde hondonada
la luz anaranjada
que la tarde deslíe
ríe.

Y abre sobre loma
su curva policroma,
el arco que ventura
augura.

Y todo azul, la hora,
tiene el alma que llora
y reza, de una santa
Infanta.

Con el rumor de un vuelo
tiembla el azul del cielo,
y un lucero florece.
Anochece.

Luis Cernuda

BAGATELA

Como un pájaro de fuego
la luna está entre las ramas
del enebro.

Negro es el cuerpo del árbol,
gris el aire nocturno,
oro el astro.

Dios por lo visto hace muestra
que ha oído de alguna estampa
japonesa.

Miguel Hernández

EN ESTE CAMPO

En este campo
estuvo el mar.

Alguna vez volverá.

Si alguna vez una gota
roza este campo, este campo
siente el recuerdo del mar.

Alguna vez volverá.

Anónimo

¡AY LUNA...!

¡Ay luna que reluces!
¡Toda la noche me alumbres!

Alúmbresme a la sierra
por do vaya y venga.

¡Ay luna que reluces!
¡Toda la noche me alumbres!

Miguel Hernández

ESCRIBÍ EN EL ARENAL

Escribí en el arenal
los tres nombres de la vida:
vida, muerte, amor.

Una ráfaga de mar,
tantas claras veces ida,
vino y los borró.

JAIME FERRÁN

LA PLAYA LARGA

Tendido junto al mar
cierro los ojos
y hasta la oscuridad
se vuelve oro,
mientras las olas suenan
cercanas,
como
una gran caracola
donde está todo.

Vicente Aleixandre

LA HERMANILLA

Tenía la naricilla respingona, y era menuda.
¡Cómo le gustaba correr por la arena!
Y se metía en el agua,
y nunca se asustaba.
Flotaba allí como si aquel hubiera sido siempre
su natural elemento.
Como si las olas la hubieran acercado a la orilla,
trayéndola desde lejos inocente en la espuma,
con ojos abiertos bajo la luz.

Rodaba luego con la onda sobre la arena
y se reía, risa de niña
en la risa del mar,
y se ponía de pie, mojada, pequeñísima,
como recién salida de las valvas de nácar,
y se adentraba en la tierra,
como en préstamo de las olas.

¿Te acuerdas?
Cuéntame lo que hay allí en el fondo del mar.
Dime, dime, yo le pedía.
No recordaba nada.
Y riendo se metía otra vez en el agua,
y se tendía sumisamente sobre las olas.

Francisco de Quevedo

LOS NADADORES

(Fragmento)

Al agua nadadores,
nadadores al agua,
alto a guardar la ropa
que en eso está la gala.

Zambúllete, chiquilla,
que por chica y delgada,
pasarás por anchoa
para las ensaladas.

¡Oh!, cómo se chapuzan,
qué sueltos se abalanzan,
y con el rostro y brazos
las corrientes apartan.

Ya nadan de bracete,
ya solo un brazo sacan;
ya, como segadores,
cortan la espuma blanca.

De espaldas dan la vuelta,
hechos ramos las palmas;
la vuelta de la trucha,
es la mejor mudanza.

Llegan al remolino,
juntos los arrebata,
las olas se los sorben,
las ondas los levantan.

LOPE DE VEGA

PIRAGUAMONTE, PIRAGUA...

Piraguamonte, piragua,
piragua, jevizarizagua.
Bío, Bío,
que mi tambo[1] le tengo en el río.

Yo me era niña pequeña,
y enviáronme un domingo
a mariscar por la playa
del río de Bío Bío;
cestillo al brazo llevaba
de plata y oro tejido.
Bío, Bío,
que mi tambo le tengo en el río.
Piraguamonte, piragua,
piragua, jevizarizagua.
 Piraguamonte, piragua,
piragua, jevizarizagua.
Bío, Bío,
que mi tambo le tengo en el río.

---

[1] tambo: posada; venta.

III

LA VERDE OLIVA

RAFAEL ALBERTI

CANCIÓN

Abrió la flor del cardón
y el campo se iluminó.

Los caballos se encendieron.
Todo se encendió.

Las vacas de luz pacían
pastizales de fulgor.

Del río brotaban barcas
de sol.

De mi corazón, ardiendo
otro corazón.

ANÓNIMO

DEL ROSAL SALE LA ROSA...

Del rosal sale la rosa.
¡Oh, qué hermosa!
¡Qué color saca tan fino!
Aunque nace del espino
nace entera y olorosa.
Nace de nuevo primor
esta flor,
huele tanto desde el suelo
que penetra hasta el cielo
su fuerza maravillosa.

RAFAEL ALBERTI

VAIVÉN

Por la noche, ya al subir,
por la tarde, ya al bajar,
yo quiero pisar la nieve
azul de jacarandá.

¿Es azul, noche delante?
¿Es lila, tarde detrás?
Yo quiero pisar la nieve
azul de jacarandá.

Si el pájaro serio canta
que es azul su azulear,
yo quiero pisar la nieve
azul de jacarandá.

Si el mirlo liliburlero,
que es lila su lilear,
yo quiero pisar la nieve
azul de jacarandá.

Ya nieve azul a la ida,
nieve lila al retornar;
yo quiero pisar la nieve
azul de jacarandá.

Mauricio Bacarisse

VILANOS

Estrellas del último
cielo de verano,
vilanitos tenues,
vilanitos claros.

Por el campo verde
de oro recamado,
¿a dónde vais ágiles,
sutiles y rápidos?

Tarde de septiembre
que dora los álamos,
y lleva estorninos
al viñedo grávido
de sombra y dulzura,
de sabrosos gajos...
(contra la bandada
vuelan los vilanos).

¿Dónde vais, pequeños,
pueriles y pálidos,
pajes del invierno,
farolillos blancos?

¡Ay, ciencia del mundo!
¡Códice miniado
de las verdes huertas
de frutos lozanos!
(Los capitulares
vense dibujados
al volver las norias
los ciegos caballos).

En la tarde azul,
de cercos dorados,
¿por qué vais tan aprisa,
pequeños vilanos?

¿Queréis daros cuenta
o saber de algo
del pobre universo,
y vais hacia el santo
colegio celeste
a clase de párvulos?

ÁNGELA FIGUERA AYMERICH

CHOPOS

Magníficos obeliscos,
chopos de la carretera,
de Soria; chopos ingentes
de fronda oscura y espesa;
rectos de la tierra al cielo
    en majestuosa hilera.

¡Qué bien montabais la guardia,
    firmes, sobre la cuneta!

Yo os pasaba la revista
    como si fuera una reina.

FEDERICO GARCÍA LORCA

AL CHOPO.
IN MEMORIAM

Dulce chopo,
dulce chopo,
te has puesto
de oro.
Ayer estabas verde,
un verde loco
de pájaros
gloriosos.
Hoy estás abatido
bajo el cielo de agosto
como yo bajo el cielo
de mi espíritu rojo.
La fragancia cautiva
de tu tronco
vendrá a mi corazón
piadoso.

¡Rudo abuelo del prado!
Nosotros
nos hemos puesto
de oro.

Jaime Ferrán

EL COLIBRÍ

Brillante
colibrí
colibrillante,
cuyo
brillo
un
instante
comprendí.

Un
día
me
cantaste
en
guaraní
tu
canción
de
diamante,

en
la
orilla
del
río
Llavarí.

Hoy
la
cantas
aquí.

JUAN RAMÓN JIMÉNEZ

VERDE, VERDEROL

Verde, verderol,
¡endulza la puesta del sol!

Palacio de encanto,
el pinar tardío
arrulla con llanto
la huida del río.
Allí el nido umbrío
tiene el verderol.

Verde, verderol,
¡endulza la puesta del sol!

La última brisa
es suspiradora;
el sol rojo irisa
al pino que llora.
¡Vaga y lenta hora
nuestra, verderol!

Verde, verderol,
¡endulza la puesta del sol!

Soledad y calma;
silencio y grandeza.
La choza del alma
se encoge y reza.
Y de pronto, ¡oh belleza!,
canta el verderol.

Su canto enajena
(¿Se ha parado el viento?)
El campo se llena
de su sentimiento.
Malva es el lamento,
verde el verderol.

Verde, verderol,
¡endulza la puesta del sol!

Gabriel Celaya

EL RUISEÑOR

(Del cantar popular vasco)

¡Cómo canta el ruiseñor en verano!
¡Siempre más allá! ¡Allá!
¡Cómo calla en el invierno cuando todo le falta!
¡Ay, ay, ay!
Nunca veo al ruiseñor, pero siempre oigo su voz.
¿Fue ayer? ¿Fue hoy?
¡Ah, cuando canta en el bosque!
¡Ah, si es de noche,
plata entre robles!
Calla, calla, ruiseñor, que si no te cazarán.
¡Ay, salva tu libertad!
No te lamentes. No cantes. Ocúltate en el zarzal.
Sé secreto. Vive en paz.

Adriano del Valle

LA DIVINA PASTORA

Canción del cuclillo tartamudo

El cuclillo tartamudo
su canción tartamudea,
y de un trébol de tres hojas
hace un rabel de tres cuerdas.

Pastora, tora, tú tienes
rebaños, baños, de ovejas…
Yo taño, taño, mi trébol
roto, roto, en la arboleda.

Su tijera envuelta en chispas
afilan afiladores,
dándole al pedal de plata
de un clavel de ruiseñores.

Dedales, dales, de plata,
y en raso rosa con perlas
pespuntes, puntes, de agujas,
con sartas, sartas, de estrellas.
Bastidores, dores, tienes
y tienes, tienes, tijeras
que abiertas, biertas, parecen,
volando, lando, cigüeñas.
Tijeras, jeras que cortan
los vientos, vientos que vuelan,
bordados, dados, los vientos
de blancas, blancas, cigüeñas.

La Pastora, a un rabadán:
—Rabadán, rabadancillo,
dime qué canta el cuclillo.

Anónimo

ÁNSARES Y ANSARINOS, ¡AHÉ!

Rodrigo Martínez,
a las ánsares, ¡ahé!
Pensando qu'eran[1] vacas
silbábalas: ¡he!

Rodrigo Martínez,
atán garridó,
los tus ansarinos,
llévalos el río, ¡ahé!
Pensando qu'eran vacas
silbábalas: ¡hc!

Rodrigo Martínez,
atán lozanó,
los tus ansarinos
llévalos al vado, ¡ahé!
Pensando qu'eran vacas
silbábalas: ¡he!

---

[1] qu'eran: que eran.

FERNANDO VILLALÓN

SEÑORA CIGÜEÑA

Señora Cigüeña,
usted que le ha visto
desde sus alturas
correr chica y chico,
¿en la blanda paja
estaban tendidos…?

Karratrrak
karratrrak
traka trak.

Usted que en la torre
fabrica su nido
y ensucia la torre
con paja y carrizos.
¿Tiene permisión
del señor Obispo?

Karratrrak
karratrrak
traka trak.

Señora Cigüeña,
¿qué trae usted en el pico?
¿Será una serpiente?
¿Será un basilisco?
¿O será una carta
que le dio Dios mismo
y usted por los aires
volando ha traído?

Karratrrak
karratrrak
traka trak.

JUAN DE TIMONEDA

CANCIONCILLA

Paced a vuestro solaz,
la mi ovejica,
pues sois bonica.

Paced a vuestro solaz
en la majada,
cata que no comas
cosa vedada.

Cosa no usada,
grande ni chica,
pues sois bonica.

JOAQUÍN GONZÁLEZ ESTRADA

GALOPE BLANCO

Galope blanco,
potrillo loco,
te estás matando…

¿Qué dolor te ha mordido,
galope blanco,
que a los chopos del río
vas deshojando…?

Potrillo loco,
galope blanco…

¿Qué dolor te ha mordido
que corres tanto…?

Molinera una copla
lo está contando:

—«La ycgüecita blanca
que yo tenía,
se me murió en silencio
viniendo el día…».

Potrillo loco,
galope blanco,
¡hasta las piedras lloran
que hay en el campo…!

ENRIQUE DÍEZ CANEDO

LA OVEJA PERDIDA

En el monte la oveja
    quedó perdida,
—pobre ovejilla tierna—,
y han salido los lobos
    de su guarida.

En el monte la oveja
    quedó perdida,
—pobre ovejilla tierna—,
y hay zarzas en el monte
    llenas de espinas.

Por huir de los lobos
    que sueltos andan,
—pobre ovejilla tierna—,
por huir de los lobos,
    cayó en la zarza.

Por huir de la zarza,
    llena de espinas
—pobre ovejilla tierna—,
en la boca del lobo
    perdió la vida.

MANUEL MACHADO

PAISAJE ESTIVAL

Lagartija en la tapia… Fuente seca.
Cardo abrasado, ceniza,
vidrio ahumado,
amapola en el tallo peludo…

Corre una estrella…
El grillo canta oculto.
Y la arboleda dice
una frase, una sola. Y vuelve
a quedarse callada.

¿Luciérnaga o rocío?
Asierra la cigarra
el silencio.

Entre los tallos del jardín, sabemos
—verde también— la víbora.

PEDRO SALINAS

CIGARRA QUE ESTÁS CANTANDO

Cigarra que estás cantando
en un rincón ignorado
del árbol que me da sombra,
no tengo ningún deseo
de saber cuál es la rama,
de tantas que me cobijan,
en que apoyas tu cantar.
Y no me importa si existes,
y no me importa si existe
algo más que ese vaivén
de tu lanzadera, esos
hilillos áureos y tensos
con que tejes el cordaje
de ese barco mañanero
de la mañana de agosto,
barco de los rumbos dulces
que no lleva a ningún puerto.

JOSÉ HIERRO

CANCIÓN

Hay que salir al aire,
¡de prisa!
tocando nuestras flautas,
alzando nuestros soles,
quemando la alegría.

Hay que irradiar el día,
apresurar el paso,
¡de prisa!,
antes que se nos eche
la noche encima.

Hay que salir al aire,
desatar la alegría,
llenar el universo
con nuestras vidas,
decir nuestra palabra
porque tenemos prisa.
Y hay muchas cosas nuestras
que acaso no se digan.

Hay que invadir el día
tocando nuestras flautas,
alzando nuestros soles,
quemando la alegría.

RAFAEL ALBERTI

CANCIÓN

Creemos al hombre nuevo
cantando.

El hombre nuevo de España,
cantando.

El hombre nuevo del mundo,
cantando.

Canto esta noche de estrellas
en que estoy solo, desterrado.

Pero en la tierra no hay nadie
que está solo, si está cantando.

Al árbol lo acompañan las hojas,
y si está seco ya no es árbol.

Al pájaro, el viento, las nubes,
y si está mudo, ya no es pájaro.

Al mar lo acompañan las olas
y su canto alegre, los barcos.

Al fuego, la llama, las chispas
y hasta las sombras cuando es alto.

Nada hay solitario en la tierra.
Creemos el hombre nuevo cantando.

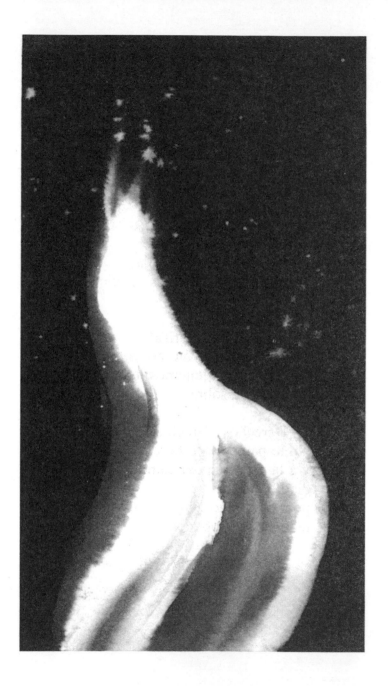

José Moreno Villa

IMPULSO

De prisa, de prisa:
lo que se cayó no lo cojas.
Tenemos más, tenemos más;
tenemos de sobra.

¡De prisa! ¡De prisa!
Lo que nos robaron, no importa.
Tenemos más, tenemos más;
tenemos de sobra.

¡Derechos, derechos!...
No te pares; coge la rosa
y a la mendiga del camino
dale la bolsa;
porque, amigo, tenemos más;
tenemos de sobra.

IV

HERMOSA TIERRA
DE ESPAÑA

BLAS DE OTERO

LO TRAIGO ANDADO

Pueblos, ríos de España, acudid
al papel, andad
en voz baja bajo la pluma; álamos,
no os mováis de la orilla
de mi mano…
            Monte
Aragón, cúpula pura, danos
la paz.

Morella, uña mellada.

Peñafiel, Fuensaldaña.

Esla. Guadalquivir. ¡Viva Sevilla!

Lo traigo andado;
cara como la suya
no la he encontrado.

Anónimo

COPLAS DE TODA ESPAÑA

España bella.
Norte en vela.

Vexo a Vigo, vexo a Vigo.
Temén vexo Compostela;
vexo o ponte de San Payo,
camiño de miñanterra.

Galicia es la huerta,
y Ponferrada la puerta.
Llueva o no llueva,
trigo en Orihuela.

Villaviciosa hermosa,
qué llevas dentro
que me llevas el alma
y el pensamiento.

Rosas y flores
en tu jardín los tienes,
verdes, azules,
de mil colores.

Quisiera cantar a Asturias
con el aire de sus fiestas,
y poner en cada nota
un recuerdo de mi aldea.

Desde Santoña a Laredo
me tengo de pasear,
porque tengo una morena
en cada puerto de mar.

No llay en España
puente colgante
más elegante
que el de Bilbao.
Porque lo han hecho
los bilbaínos,
que son muy finos
y muy salaos.

Valle de Esla,
donde yo nací;
entre tus montañas
¡qué alegre es vivir!

Campana, la de Toledo;
iglesia, la de León;
reloj, el de Benavente,
y rollo, el de Villalón.

En Madrid, el que madruga
se levanta de mañana,
almuerza si tiene qué
y come si tiene gana.

La Puerta de Toledo
tiene una cosa:
que se abre y se cierra
como las otras.

De Madrid a Toledo
hay doce leguas;
el galán que las ande
no duerme en ellas.

Carretera de Madrid
un carretero cantaba
al son de las campanillas
que sus mulitas llevaban.

Estella, la bella;
Pamplona, la bona;
Olite y Tafalla,
la flor de Navarra.

¡Qué gusto es en Zaragoza
oír a un niño cantar
con la bandurria tocando
si serena noche está!

Aunque la Mancha tenga
dos mil lugares,
no hay otro más alegre
que Manzanares.

Montanyes regalades
son les del Canigó,
que tot l'estiu floreixen
primavera i tardor.

El cielo de Andalucía
está vestido de azul;
por eso la sal abunda
en todo el cielo andaluz.

¡Sevilla del alma mía!
¡Sevilla de mi consuelo!
¡Quién estuviera en Sevilla,
aunque durmiera en el suelo!

Viva Cádiz porque tiene
las murallas hacia el mar
y veinticinco cañones
apuntando a Gibraltar.

Tres cosas tiene Granada
que no las tiene Madrid:
El Albaicín, la Alhambra
y el Puente del Genil.

Cartagena me da pena
y Murcia me da dolor.
¡Cartagena de mi vida!
¡Murcia de mi corazón!

Para aceitunas, Sevilla;
para turrón, Alicante;
para flores, Barcelona,
y para puerto, Cádiz.

Viva Valencia y Murviedro
y Castellón de la Plana;
vivan los reales saleros
de las chicas valencianas.

Alicante, por su muelle;
Murcia, por sus arrabales;
Orihuela, por su huerta;
Elche, por sus palmerales.

El mundo tiene una Europa.
Europa tiene una España,
y España tiene un jardín,
que son las islas Canarias.

José García Nieto

LÍMITES CONVENCIONALES

España limita al norte...
¡Arqueros, pronto, apuntad!
Flecha la de Santa Clara,
arco el de San Sebastián.
Al oeste, yo te he visto,
siempre verde, Portugal,
repartirte el río Tajo
y ensancharlo hasta estallar.
Al este, Calpe hacia Roma,
antiguo Peñón de Ifach.
Y al sur, al sur no lo olvido,
aunque no lo vea más:
un león arrodillado
que no come nuestra sal,
un león vuelto de espaldas
que se llama Gibraltar.

RAFAEL ALBERTI

RUTAS

Por allí, por allá,
a Castilla se va.
Por allá, por allí,
a mi verde país.

Quiero ir por allí,
quiero ir por allá.
A la mar, por allí;
a mi hogar, por allá.

CARMEN CONDE

EL NIÑO MIRABA EL AGUA

Miño del atardecer
con dos hileras de pinos,
    ¡ay qué dulcísimo río!

Hondo entre piedras guardado
con un silencioso sino
deslizándose al encuentro
de otro río delgadísimo,
    ¡ay qué dulcísimo río!

Que salta como una corza
que se entrega a su destino,
    ¡ay qué dulcísimo río!

Manuel Machado

CANTO A ANDALUCÍA

Cádiz, salada claridad. Granada,
agua oculta que llora.
Romana y mora, Córdoba callada.
Málaga cantaora.
Almería dorada.
Plateado Jaén. Huelva, la orilla
de las tres carabelas.

Y Sevilla...

MIGUEL DE UNAMUNO

ARROYUELO SIN NOMBRE…

Arroyuelo sin nombre ni historia
que a la sombra del roble murmuras
bañando sus raíces,
¿quién llama a tus aguas?

Al nacer en la cumbre, en el cielo,
con el monte sueñas,
con el mar que en el cielo se acuesta,
¡arroyuelo sin nombre ni historia!

Miguel de Unamuno

ÁVILA, MÁLAGA, CÁCERES

Ávila, Málaga, Cáceres,
Játiva, Mérida, Córdoba,
Ciudad Rodrigo, Sepúlveda,
Úbeda, Arévalo, Frómista,
Zumárraga, Salamanca,
Turégano, Zaragoza,
Lérida, Zamarramala,
Arrancudiaga, Zamora.
Sois nombres de cuerpo entero,
libres, propios, los de nómina,
el tuétano intraductible
de nuestra lengua española.

BLAS DE OTERO

EN EL NOMBRE DE ESPAÑA, PAZ

En el nombre de España, paz.
El hombre
está en peligro. España,
España, no te
aduermas.
Está en peligro, corre,
acude. Vuela
el ala de la nochc
junto al ala del día.
Oye.
Cruje una vieja sombra,
vibra una luz joven.
Paz
para el día.
          En el nombre
de España, paz.

LOPE DE VEGA

CANCIÓN DE ROMERÍA

Vuela, caballito, vuela:
darte he yo cebada nueva.

Hicieron su agosto
por aquestas vegas,
en donde se juntan
y casados quedan
Manzanares verde
y Jarama bella.
Los pastores suyos,
después de la siega,
y de espigas rojas
una cruz compuesta,
vienen a la ermita,
quieren ofrecerla.

Vuela, caballito, vuela:
darte he yo cebada nueva.

A Santa María,
rosa madreselva;
a su hijo hermoso,
lirios y azucenas;
a San Juan Bautista,
olorosas hierbas;
a San Pedro Apóstol,
mastranzo y verbena;
a San Roque hermoso,
trigo de las eras;
a San Sebastián,
trébol y mosquetas;
al gran San Cristóbal,
pinos de la sierra.

Vuela, caballito, vuela:
darte he yo cebada nueva.

Concha Zardoya

CANCIONCILLAS DE AUSENCIAS

LA MIEL DE LA ALCARRIA HUELE

La miel de la Alcarria huele,
mis amigas.
¡La miel blanca de la Alcarria!
¡Dorado olor a nostalgia!

(Alcarria)

VIENTO DE ABRIL

Viento de abril,
en el Genil,
flor de alhelí
llora por ti.

(Granada)

CÓMO SE QUEJA EL VIENTO

¡Cómo se queja el viento
cuando muere algún niño,
cuando muere algún sueño!

MI PATRIA ES UN VIENTO

Mi patria es un viento
que no tiene dueño
en el mar abierto.
Mi patria es un sueño
que duerme en mi pecho
con ojos eternos.

Anónimo

LAS VÍRGENES ESPAÑOLAS

Guadalupe, en Extremadura;
en Aragón, el Pilar;
en Asturias, Covadonga,
y en Cataluña, Montserrat.

A la Virgen del Camino,
Patrona de la región,
defendió estas provincias
desde el reino de León.

La de Atocha está en Madrid;
la del Sagrario, en Toledo,
y la Virgen del Pilar,
a la orillica del Ebro.

La Virgen de la Paloma
le dijo a la del Pilar:
—Si tú eres zaragozana,
yo madrileña inmortal.

Rafael Montesinos

ROMANCILLO DE LA ESPERANZA
DE TRIANA

La Virgen duda,
llena de gracia,
si nazarena,
si sevillana.

Cirios tendidos,
túnicas blancas,
cien capirotes
sobre cien capas.
Ya por San Pablo
la Virgen pasa
(la Cruz de Guía,
por la Campana).

Si nazarena,
si sevillana.

Porque es ahora
Semana Santa,
bajo su palio
va por la plaza
entre varales
de sueño y plata
(gritan y rezan,
rezan y cantan).

Si nazarena,
si sevillana.

Porque de Egipto
no se acordaba
y ahora se acuerda,
pasa callada,
entre sus dudas
inauguradas
(dudas de Niña
Virgen mimada).

Si las Pirámides,
si la Giralda.

Por San Jacinto,
de madrugada,
lejos del Puente,
pasa callada
(hoy no se acuesta
nadie en Triana).

La Virgen duda,
frente a su casa.

Si trianera,
si sevillana.

V

ROMANCES

ROMANCES VIEJOS

EL CONDE ARNALDOS

¡Quién hubiese tal ventura
sobre las aguas de mar
como hubo el conde Arnaldos
la mañana de San Juan!
     Con un falcón[1] en la mano
la caza iba cazar,
vio venir una galera
que a tierra quiere llegar.
     Las velas traía de seda,
la jarcia de un cendal,
marinero que la manda
diciendo viene un cantar
que la mar facía en calma,

---

[1] falcón: halcón.

los vientos hace amainar,
los peces que andan'nel[2] hondo
arriba los hace andar,
las aves que andan volando
en el mástil las face posar.
    Allí fabló[3] el conde Arnaldos,
bien oiréis lo que dirá:
    —Por Dios te ruego, marinero,
dígasme ora ese cantar.
    Respondióle el marinero,
tal respuesta le fue a dar:
    —Yo no digo esta canción
sino a quien conmigo va.

---

[2] andan'nel: andan en el.
[3] fabló: habló.

LA NIÑA ADORMECIDA

La mañana de San Juan
tres horas antes del día,
salíme yo a pasear
por una huerta florida.
En medio de aquella huerta
un alto ciprés había,
el tronco tenía de oro,
las ramas de plata fina.
A la sombra del ciprés
vide sentada una niña,
mata de pelo tiene
que todo el prado cubría,
con peine de oro en la mano
lo peinaba y lo tejía,
luego que lo hubo peinado
la niña se adormecía.
Ha bajado un ruiseñor
con alegre cantoría,
y posado se ha en el pecho
de la niña adormecida.

LA MISA MAYOR

Mañanita de San Juan,
mañanita de primor,
cuando damas y galanes
van a oír misa mayor.
Allá va la mi señora,
entre todas la mejor;
viste saya sobre saya,
mantillo de tornasol[1],
camisa con oro y perlas,
bordada en el cabezón[2];
en la su boca muy linda
lleva un poco de dulzor;
en la su cara tan blanca
un poquito de arrebol,
y en los sus ojuelos garzos[3]
lleva un poco de alcohol[4];
así entraba en la iglesia
relumbrando como el sol.

---

[1] tornasol: con reflejos.
[2] cabezón: abertura para sacar la cabeza.
[3] garzos: de color azulado.
[4] alcohol: polvo para oscurecer los párpados y las pestañas.

Las damas mueren de envidia
y los galanes de amor;
el que cantaba en el coro
en el credo se perdió;
el abad que dice misa
no la puede decir, non;
monaguillos que le ayudan
no aciertan responder, non;
por decir amén, amén,
decían amor, amor.

ROMANCES DE TRADICIÓN ORAL MODERNA

DONCELLA GUERRERA

En Sevilla a un sevillano
gran desgracia le dio Dios,
de siete hijos que tuvo,
ninguno fue varón.
　　—Padre, deme usted caballo
que a la guerra me voy yo.
　　—Tienes el pelo muy largo
para ser hombre varón.
　　—Yo lo esconderé, padre,
debajo de mi morrión.
　　—Tienes los pechos muy altos
para ser hombre y varón.
　　—Yo lo esconderé, padre,
debajo de mi jubón.
　　Siete años fue a la guerra,
nadie que la conoció,
un día al subir al caballo
la espada se le cayó,
dijo: —Maldita sea la espada,
y maldita sea yo.
　　El Rey, que la estaba oyendo,
de ella se enamoró:

—Madrecita de mi alma,
que yo me muero de amor;
que el caballero Don Marco
es hembra, que no varón.
　　—Convídale tú, hijo mío,
a comer contigo un día,
que si ella fuera mujer
en bajo se sentaría.
　　—Los tres caballeros, madre,
se sientan en lo más bajo,
el caballero Don Marco
se ha sentado en lo más alto.
　　—Convídale tú, hijo mío,
a correr contigo un día,
que si ella es mujer
al punto se cansaría.
　　—Los tres caballeros, madre,
pronto se han retirado,
el caballero Don Marco
delante de mí ha pasado.

DONCELLA GUERRERA

Un capitán sevillano
siete hijas le dio Dios,
y tuvo la mala suerte
que ninguno fue varón.
Un día la más pequeña
le cayó la inclinación
de que se fuera a la guerra
vestidita de varón.
—Hija, no vayas, no vayas
que te van a conocer,
llevas el pelo muy largo
y dirán que eres mujer.

—Padre, si lo llevo largo
padre, córtemelo usted,
que con el pelo cortado
un varón pareceré.
  Siete años en la guerra
y nadie la conoció.
  Un día al subir a caballo
la espada se le cayó,
y en vez de decir maldito,
dijo, ¡maldita sea yo!
  El rey que la estaba oyendo
a palacio la llevó;
arreglaron los papeles
y con ella se casó.
  Aquí se acaba la historia
de la niña y el varón.

VUELTA DEL MARIDO

Estaba ahora Catalina
sentada bajo un laurel
contemplando la hermosura
de las aguas al caer.
De pronto pasó un soldado
y ella lo hizo detener.

—Deténgase usted, soldado,
que una pregunta le haré,
la pregunta que yo le hago,
la pregunta que yo haré,
¿si ha visto a mi marido
en la guerra alguna vez?

—Yo no he visto a su marido,
ni lo puedo conocer,
yo no he visto a su marido
en la guerra alguna vez.

—Mi marido es alto y rubio,
tan buen mozo como usted,
y en la cinta del sombrero
lleva escrito San Andrés.

—Su marido ha muerto en guerra,
su marido muerto fue,
y me ha dado a mí el encargo
que me case con usted.
    —Si ha muerto mi marido
con nadie me casaré.
A los tres hijos varones
a la guerra mandaré
y a las dos hijas mujeres
conmigo las quedaré.
    —Calla, calla, Catalina,
calla, calla, de una vez
que estás viendo a tu marido
y no lo sabes conocer.

VUELTA DEL MARIDO

—Soldadito, soldadito.
¿De dónde ha venido usted?
  —He venido de la guerra,
de la guerra de Aranjuez.
  —¿Ha visto usted a mi marido
una vez en Aranjuez?
  —Si le he visto no me acuerdo:
deme usted las señas de él.
  —Mi marido es alto y rubio,
alto y rubio aragonés,
en la punta de la lanza
lleva un pañuelo bordés,
se lo bordé cuando niña,
cuando niña lo bordé;
uno que le estoy bordando
y otro que le bordaré.
Siete años llevo esperando,
y otros siete esperaré,
si a los catorce no viene
monjita me meteré.
  —Calla, Isabelita, calla,
calla, por Dios, Isabel,
que soy tu querido esposo,
tú mi querida mujer.

LAS TRES CAUTIVAS

En el campo moro,
entre las olivas,
allí cautivaron
tres niñas perdidas;
el pícaro moro
que las cautivó
a la reina mora
se las entregó.
—Toma, reina mora,
estas tres cautivas,
para que te valgan,
para que te sirvan.
—¿Cómo se llamaban?,
¿cómo les decían?
—La mayor Constanza,
la menor Lucía,
y la más chiquita,
la llaman María.
Constanza amasaba,
Lucía cernía,
y la más chiquita
agua les traía.

Un día en la fuente,
en la fuente fría,
con un pobre viejo,
se halló la más niña.
 —¿Dónde vas, buen viejo,
camina, camina?
 —Así voy buscando
a mis tres hijitas.
 —¿Cómo se llamaban?,
¿cómo les decían?
 —La mayor Constanza,
la menor Lucía,
y la más pequeña,
se llama María.
 —Usted es mi padre.
 —¡Tú eres mi hija!
 —Yo voy a contarlo
a mis hermanitas.
 —¿No sabes, Constanza,
no sabes, Lucía,
que he encontrado a padre
en la fuente fría?
Constanza lloraba,
lloraba Lucía,
y la más pequeña
de gozo reía.

HERMANA CAUTIVA

El día de los monteros
pasé por la morería,
y vi una mora lavando
al pie de una fuente fría.
   —Retírate, mora bella,
retírate, mora linda,
deja que beba el caballo
en estas aguas cristalinas.
   —No soy mora, caballero,
que soy cristiana cautiva,
me cautivaron los moros
desde chiquitina y niña.
   —¿Te quieres venir conmigo
en esta caballería?
   —De buena gana me iría,
mas los pañuelos que yo lavo
¿dónde yo los dejaría?
   —Los de seda y los de holanda
en esta caballería,
los que estén un poquito rotos,
la corriente los llevaría.

Al pasar por aquel bosque
la morita llora y suspira.
—¿Por qué suspiras, morita?
—Suspiro porque me encuentro
donde yo he sido nacida.
Mi padre buen rey,
mi madre la reina,
sentadita en silla,
sentadita en silla,
mi hermano don Juan
los toros corría.
—¡Abrid puertas, madre,
puertas de alegría,
por traeros nuera
traigo vuestra hija!
—Para ser mi hija,
qué descolorida.
—Qué queréis, señora,
si nada comía,
si no eran berros
de una fuente fría,
si no eran berros
de una fuente helada.

DELGADINA

Un rey tenía tres hijas
y las tres como la plata,
la más rechiquitita
Delgadina se llamaba.
Un día estando comiendo
su padre la remiraba.
—Padre mío de mi alma,
¿qué mira usted a la cara?
—Que te tengo de mirar
que has de ser mi enamorada.
—No lo consienta Dios
ni la Virgen Santa Clara,
ser la mujer de mi padre
y madre de mis hermanas.
Granaderos, granaderos,
los que traje de Granada,
a mi hija Delgadina
encerradla en una sala;
no me la deis de comer
sino es cecina salada,
no me la deis de beber
sino son hieles amargas.

Pasan días, pasan días,
ya se asoma a una ventana;
desde allí vio a su hermana
que en juego de pelota estaba.
 —Hermanita de mi vida,
hermanita de mi alma,
por aquel que hay en la Cruz
súbeme una jarra de agua.
 —Bien te la subiera, hija,
bien te la subiera, hermana,
pero si una gota subo
he de morir arrastrada.
 Pasan días, pasan días,
ya se asoma a otra más alta;
desde allí vio a su hermano
que en juego de brincar estaba.
 —Hermanito de mi vida,
hermanito de mi alma,
por aquel que hay en la Cruz
súbeme una jarra de agua.

Bien te la subiera, perra,
bien te la subiera, malvada,
pero no has querido hacer
lo que padre rey mandaba.
    Pasan días, pasan días,
ya se asoma a otra más alta;
desde allí vio a su padre
que en el jardín paseaba.
    —Padre mío de mi vida,
padre mío de mi alma,
por aquel que hay en la Cruz
súbeme una jarra de agua,
con el corazón la pido
ya la vida se me acaba.
    Granaderos, granaderos,
los que traje de Granada,
a mi hija la Delgadina
subidla una jarra de agua.

Unos con jarras de oro,
otros, con jarras de plata;
cuando el agua ya subiera,
la Delgadina expiraba.
Los ángeles la sostenían,
la Virgen la amortajaba;
las campanas ellas solas,
solitas repicaban,
en la cama de su hermana,
llena de ángeles estaba,
en la cama de su hermano,
una serpiente enroscada,
en la cama de su padre,
los demonios la llevaban.

MONJITA A LA FUERZA

Una tarde de verano
me llevaron de paseo;
al pasar por una esquina
me encontré con un convento.
Desde allí salió una monja
toda vestida de negro,
con una cruz en la mano
que parecía un entierro.
Me sentaron en la sillita,
me cortaron la melena,
anillito de mis dedos,
pulseras de mi muñeca,
gargantilla de mi cuello,
polisón de mi cadera.

ROMANCILLO DE LOS PEREGRINITOS

Para Roma caminan
dos peregrinos,
a que los case el Papa
porque son primos.
Lleva la peregrina
sombrero negro
y el peregrinito
de terciopelo.
Al pasar el arroyo
de la Victoria,
tropezó la madrina,
cayó la novia.
Han llegado a Palacio,
suben arriba,
y en la sala del Papa
los examinan.
Le ha preguntado el Papa
cómo se llaman,
él le dice que Pedro,
ella que Ana.

Le ha preguntado el Papa
que qué edad tienen,
ella dice que quince
y él, diecisiete.

Le ha preguntado el Papa
de dónde eran,
ella dice: —De Cabra.
Y él: —De Antequera.

Le ha preguntado el Papa
que si han pecado.

—Al pasar el arroyo
le di un abrazo.

Las campanas de Roma
ya repicaron,
porque los peregrinos
ya se casaron.

HIJAS DE MERINO

—Papá si me deja ir
un ratito a la alameda,
con las hijas de Merino
que llevan rica merienda.
    A la hora de comer,
se perdió la más pequeña.
Su papá la fue a buscar
calle arriba, calle abajo,
¿dónde la fue a encontrar?
En un portalito oscuro
hablando con su galán,
y estas palabras decía:
    —Contigo me he de casar
aunque me cueste la vida.

DON GATO

Estaba el señor don Gato,
estaba el señor don Gato,
en silla de oro sentado,
miau, miau, mirrimiau,
en silla de oro sentado,
calzando medias de seda
y zapatito dorado,
cuando llegó la noticia
que debía ser casado
con una gatita parda,
hija de un gato romano.
    El gato con la alegría,
se cayó desde el tejado;

se rompió siete costillas
y la puntita del rabo.
Llamaron a los médicos,
médicos y cirujanos;
mataron siete gallinas
y le dieron de aquel caldo.
Ya le llevan a enterrar
al pobrecito don Gato,
y le llevan en hombros
cuatro gatos colorados.
   Ya lo llevan a enterrar
por la calle del Pescado;
al olor de las sardinas
el gato ha resucitado,
miau, miau, mirrimiau.

HILO DE ORO

Hilo de oro, hilo de plata,
hilito de San Gabriel,
que me ha dicho una señora
que lindas hijas tenéis.
    —Si las tengo o no las tengo
yo las sabré mantener,
con el pan que Dios me ha dado
comen ellas y yo también.
    —Yo me voy muy enojado
a los palacios del rey,
a contárselo a la reina
y al hijo del rey también.
    —Vuelva, vuelva, pastorcillo,
no sea tan descortés,
de las tres hijas que tengo
escoja la que quiera usted.
    —Esta escojo por galana,
esta escojo por mujer,
parece una rosa
acabada de nacer.

Bibliografía

- Alberti, Rafael. «Canción», p. 84; «Vaivén», p. 78; «Canción», p. 149; «Rutas», p. 159: en *Poesía española para niños*. Madrid, Taurus, 1993.
- Aleixandre, Vicente. «La hermanilla», p. 35: en *Poesía española para niños*. Madrid, Taurus, 1993.
- Alonso, Dámaso. «Calle del arrabal», p. 58: en *Poesía española para niños*. Madrid, Taurus, 1993.
- Anónimo. «Teresilla hermana, hermano Perico», «Morenica me era», «Ánsares y ansarinos, ¡ahé!», «El conde Arnaldos», «Doncella guerrera», «Vuelta del marido», «Hermana cautiva», «Monjita a la fuerza», «Hijas de Merino», «Hilo de oro».
- —. «Sol, sol...», p. 130; «Cancioncilla del donaire», p. 29; «Tres morillas me enamoran», p. 32; «En esta plazuelita...», p. 54; «¡Ay luna...!», p. 66; «Del rosal sale la rosa...», p. 78; «Coplas de toda España», p. 154; «La niña adormecida», p. 174; «La misa mayor», p. 182; «Doncella guerrera», p. 171; «Vuelta del marido», p. 175; «Las tres cautivas», p. 173; «Delgadina», p. 176; «Romancillo de los peregrinitos», p. 181; «Don Gato», p. 183: en *Poesía española para niños*. Madrid, Taurus, 1993.
- —. «Las vírgenes españolas», p. 154: en *Poesía española para niños. Antología*. Madrid, Taurus, 1979.
- Bacarisse, Mauricio. «Vilanos», p. 82: en *Poesía española para niños*. Madrid, Taurus, 1993.
- Celaya, Gabriel. «Ruiseñor»: en *Obras Completas*. Madrid, Editorial Aguilar, 1968.
- Cernuda, Luis. «Málibu», p. 336; «Bagatela», p. 330: en *La realidad y el deseo* [1936], México. Fondo de Cultura Económica, 1985.
- Conde, Carmen. «El niño miraba el agua», p. 24: en *Canciones de nana y desvelo*. Madrid, Miñón-Susaeta, 1985.
- Diego, Gerardo. «San Baudelio de Berlanga», p. 40: en *Poesía española para niños*. Madrid, Taurus, 1993.
- —. «Balón», p. 90: en *Gerardo Diego para niños*. Madrid, Ediciones Alba y Mayo de la Torre, 1985.
- Díez Canedo, Enrique. «La oveja perdida», p. 108: en *Poesía española para niños*. Madrid, Taurus, 1993.
- Egea, Julio Alfredo. «Nana del gitanillo», p. 5: en *Nana para dormir una muñeca*. Madrid, Editorial Nacional, 1965.
- Ferrán, Jaime. «La playa larga», p. 14: en *La playa larga*. Madrid, Miñón-Susaeta, 1981.
- —. «Ciclistas», p. 28: en *Tarde de circo*. Madrid, Miñón-Susaeta, 1966.
- —. «El colibrí», p. 73: en *Mañana de parque*. Madrid, Editorial Anaya, 1972.
- Figuera Aymerich, Ángela. «Siesta», p. 55; «Chopos», p. 86: en *Poesía española para niños*. Madrid, Taurus, 1993.
- García Lorca, Federico. «Paisaje», p. 54; «Canción primaveral», p. 47; «Al chopo. *In memoriam*», p. 85: en *Poesía española para niños*. Madrid, Taurus, 1993.

- García Nieto, José. «Límites convencionales», p. 159: en *Poesía española para niños*. Madrid, Taurus, 1993.
- González Estrada, Joaquín. «Galope blanco», p. 36: en *Monigote pintado*. Madrid, Miñón-Susaeta, 1982.
- Guillén, Jorge. «Soledades», p. 66; «Manera actual de ser niño», p. 45: en *Niños*. Málaga, Begar ediciones. Poesía; Colección dirigida por Dionisio García y J. Salvador Becerra, 1983.
- Hernández, Miguel. «Escribí en el arenal», p. 37; «En este campo», p. 27: en *Miguel Hernández para niños*. Madrid. Ediciones de la Torre, 1979.
- Hierro, José. «Caballero de otoño», p. 60; «Canción», p. 148: en *Poesía española para niños*. Madrid, Taurus, 1993.
- Jiménez, Juan Ramón. «Fin de invierno», p. 56; «Verde, verderol», p. 93: en *Poesía española para niños*. Madrid, Taurus, 1993.
- Lacaci, María Elvira. «Solo sé…», p. 23: en *Molinos de papel*. Madrid, Editorial Nacional, 1968.
- Machado, Antonio. «Sol de invierno», p. 53: en *Poesía española para niños*. Madrid, Taurus, 1993.
- Machado, Manuel. «Paisaje estival»: en *Obras Completas*. Sevilla, Editorial Renacimiento, 1993.
- —. «Canto a Andalucía», p. 161: en *Poesía española para niños*. Madrid, Taurus, 1993.
- Montesinos, Rafael. «Romancillo de la Esperanza de Triana», p. 165: en *Poesía española para niños*. Madrid, Taurus, 1993.
- Moreno Villa, José. «Impulso», p. 158: en *Poesía española para niños*. Madrid, Taurus, 1993.
- Otero, Blas de. «Lo traigo andado», p. 153; «En el nombre de España, paz», p. 167: en *Poesía española para niños*. Madrid, Taurus, 1993.
- Quevedo, Francisco de. «Los nadadores» (frag.), p. 73: en *Poesía española para niños*. Madrid, Taurus, 1993.
- Salinas, Pedro. «Cigarra que estás cantando», p. 98: en *Poesía española para niños*. Madrid, Taurus, 1993.
- Timoneda, Juan de. «Cancioncilla», p. 106: en *Poesía española para niños*. Madrid, Taurus, 1993.
- Unamuno, Miguel de. «Poemas», n.° 274, n.° 1.347: en *Cancionero 1928-1936*. Madrid, Akal, 1984.
- Valle, Adriano del. «La divina pastora», p. 91: en *Poesía española para niños*. Madrid, Taurus, 1993.
- Valle-Inclán, Ramón María del. «Milagro de la mañana», p. 61; «Rosa vespertina», p. 65: en *Poesía española para niños*. Madrid, Taurus, 1993.
- Vega, Lope de. «Caballero de Panamá», p. 23; «Piraguamonte, piragua…», p. 67; «Canción de romería», p. 146: en *Poesía española para niños*. Madrid, Taurus, 1993.
- Vicente, Gil. «Cantiga», p. 30; «Gentil serrana», p. 141: en *Poesía española para niños*. Madrid, Taurus. 1993.
- Villalón, Fernando. «Señora Cigüeña», p. 94: en *Poesía española para niños*. Madrid, Taurus, 1993.
- Zardoya, Concha. «Cancioncillas de ausencias», pp. 110-111: en *Corral de vivos y muertos*. Buenos Aires, Editorial Losada, 1965.

Índice alfabético
de autores

Índice

II
ESOS DÍAS AZULES

III
LA VERDE OLIVA

IV
HERMOSA TIERRA DE ESPAÑA

V
ROMANCES

Romances viejos

Romances de tradición oral moderna

DESDE **12** AÑOS

Poesía española para jóvenes

Selección y prólogo de Ana Pelegrín

Ilustraciones de Juan Ramón Alonso

Una antología que reúne a nuestros mejores poetas en una escogida y cuidada selección, muy adecuada a la sensibilidad de los adolescentes de hoy. Rafael Alberti, Gabriel Celaya, Gerardo Diego, García Lorca, Valle-Inclán, Unamuno, José Hierro... nos hablan con sus versos del amor, de la naturaleza, del sentido de la vida.

ISBN: 978-84-204-6501-2

ALFAGUARA
JUVENIL

9 788420 465012

940191

THE DESTROYER #153: MONUMENTAL TERROR

This edition published in 2019 by Warren Murphy Media
E-book edition published in 2019 by Gere Donovan Press

ISBN-13: 9781944073688 (Destroyer Books)
ISBN-10: 194407368X

Requests for reproduction or interviews should be directed to
DestroyerBooks@gmail.com

Cover art by Gere Donovan Press/Devin Murphy

The Destroyer

153: MONUMENTAL TERROR

R.J. CARTER
CREATED BY WARREN MURPHY AND RICHARD SAPIR

For my sister, Aileen Robbins,
for reminding me, always,
that laughter is the best medicine.

CONTENTS

PART I.   2012.   BUDDHA LAUGHING

PART II.   2013.   LAUGHING LESSONS

PART III. 2014. ENDLESS LAUGHTER

FOREWORD

I knew I needed more laughter in my life, and somehow I got it into my head to buy a statue of a Laughing Buddha. I looked at and rejected many Laughing Buddhas before I found the one that inspired these poems. You can see him on the front cover and on the back.

I feel lucky that he fit so perfectly into the empty space against the back of the garage, directly across from my front door. After all, why get a statue if you're not going to be able to look at it?!

Since this book tells a story, it would be best to read it in the order it was written, in the order it appears here. I am not a Buddhist, but my reverence for and my devotion to the Laughing Buddha have turned out to be ineffably deep and profound, and have changed my life.

May this book encourage us all to laugh more, smile more. That is what my Buddha did for me, and that is the story of these poems.

Part I. 2012. Buddha Laughing

WELCOME

My sitting Buddha's stone and stalwart
Laughing by my study door --
How can I not smile?

Of course he's laughing.
Legally my study's A GARAGE;
Its outside is aluminum!

(Is nothing really what it seems
Does nothing seem like what it really is?)

Of course he's laughing:
In spite of wars and suicides and ruined crops
The sun keeps rising every morning;
Of course he's laughing: he's made of stone
But sometimes he looks human and alive,
And always
Makes me smile.

EYEBROWS

Buddha's eyebrows!
They look like flying birds.
No wonder he's laughing.

Maybe they are birds flying.
Ha, ha, ha, ha, ha, ha, ha.

BUDDHA'S HEAD

That round, round head!
It makes me smile and think of
Other globes, not only planets
But also balls to juggle:
The balls of my feet! or the balls
In the joints of my shoulders and hips!
The orbs at my elbows, my wrists and my ankles;
Or the balls in the air
Of all my electrons,
And protons
And neutrons!

Yes, let's shake things up,
Let's shake things loose,
Until my juggling body
Is a perfect circus -- clowns,
And all the children laughing.

PROPER BREAKFAST

I have breakfast with my Buddha
When I can remember.
Why? He's laughing.
Ha ha ha ha ha.
His laughter has me sit up straight!
My body wants to laugh!

Today we watch a bird
That's doing what I do not understand:
It burrows in a corner of a step
To my garage, as if to make a nest,
And my old Buddha laughs
As if he understands some cosmic joke,
Laughs even while
My best friend's stage four melanoma
Is a mystery, too, and two good friends,
Both also in New York, have lost their breasts
To cancers of their own. Is it the city?
Is it my friends? Is it our lives cut off
From the burrowing birds
And Laughing Buddhas?

Six years ago I had a tumor, too, inside my neck,
A lump as big as a little plum,
And worried it might be malignant.
This made me search for what I truly loved,

For things that really gave me joy:
I saw the book of poems I hadn't finished;
And all the people that I loved;
And when the surgery was done,
And when I learned the growth had been benign,
And when I saw I had survived --
I sobbed to see how much I loved
My Life!

DOG VISIT

I have a Laughing Buddha in my garden.
The neighbor's dog just visited
And peed all over Buddha's left hand side:
He wet my Buddha's head, his belly
And his heart,

And my Buddha's laughing
Ha, ha, ha, ha,
Ha, ha, ha, ha, ha.

ROOSTER

Yesterday I bought a metal rooster
For my garden.
The bird is painted black,
White spots for feathers,
A red comb, red wattles,
A pointy, orange beak
And feet as thin and tan as twigs,
And stood him up
Outside my study wall
A little ways from Buddha.

This afternoon I see
My bird's been toppled by the wind
So that its beak is pecking
At my Buddha's shoulder.
And Buddha's laughing,
Tickled pink.
Ha, ha, ha, ha, ha, ha, ha.

OCEAN CURE

My Laughing Buddha
Doesn't miss a thing,
He notices I'm sad
And then suggests I

"Take a drive along the coast,
Go and watch the waves,
Their white caps
Full of light
And curling up and smiling,
And laughing, yes!
Like me, laughing!"

DINNER WITH BUDDHA

I eat at my outside table,
Buddha faces me.
We laugh through dinner.
Okay, I only smile. I want to laugh,
I also want to eat.

It's hard to look at him
And not at least be smiling --
Is it just my empathetic mirror cells?
I know they make us frown with frowners,
Laugh with laughers,
Ha ha ha ha ha ha ha.
Or have I come to think of laughing
As a Spiritual Discipline!?
Whatever it is, smiling as I am,
I should digest my dinner better.

AROUND YOUR NECK

Okay --
What's with the necklace?
I know, I know, it's like a rosary
With beads to count your prayers:
One, two, three, four, five,
Ha, ha, ha, ha, ha,
Six, seven, eight, nine, ten,
Ho, ho, ho, ho, ho,

The beads all bound in one
Unending circle, each a perfect sphere --
So let me count how many
Perfect prayers of gratitude and grace
There just might be --
Surely an infinity.

RABBIT GRASS

On the ground around
My laughing Buddha
There must be special grass,
Or has my Buddha made it so,
Because the neighbor rabbits
Gobble it at breakneck speed
Their tall ears standing vertical
Just like the grasses I cut down
Soon after Buddha first arrived
(Though who knows why I did,
When such devoted cotton-tails
Devour them for breakfast, lunch and dinner!).

I watch their big brown eyes,
Glassy and wise,
Maybe watching me
Watching them;
Or maybe that's just how they look
As they nibble, chew
And chomp at life
Hungry to live.

SONG OF THE LAUGHING BUDDHA

Ha ha ha ha ha ha ha,
Heh heh heh heh heh heh heh,
Ha ha ha ha ha ha ha.

Part II.   2012.   Laughing Lessons

"HAVE FUN TODAY. LIFE'S TOO SHORT!"

"Have fun today. Life's too short,"
My friend Jack Heller says.
And on his answering machine!

In spite of this, this morning I woke up
Unhappy, worried, stalling, heavy,
And it's true, the "FUN" word
Nowhere near my mind,
Even with my Buddha right outside,
Laughing himself silly,
Laughing at me I'll bet!

You mean stop angsting about
My slow careers, my laryngitis, strep,
My dog (she's dead), HAVE FUN?
Let go the martyr mantra of my mother
And embrace my dad's philosophy of
"Have a ball, ol' gal," the way he always
Signed his postcards and his letters?

YES! So let me hug a child, or eat a sweet,
Or watch a rabbit running in the field,
Or if there isn't one, enjoy the rabbit
Made of stone I ordered from a catalogue
And placed behind the sage bush in my garden --
(My very own Versailles with one stone statue!).

HAVE FUN?! Another F word --
Hotter than "fuck," much more of a challenge,
Less angry, much less complicated,
Plus it is our nature to be joyful and to play --
Watch young children, even in a crib!
And I forgot! But how?

Has our Zeitgeist held me hostage
In its cave of wars, deceit and angst?
THEN LET ME OUT
AND INTO THE SUNLIGHT!
Let me play with a big red rubber ball
Or go see a movie and have real buttered popcorn,
Or roll and roll down a thick, grassy hillside,
Or laugh so hard the tears roll down my cheeks
And follow your example, Laughing Buddha,
And even laugh with you.

Okay, I'm smiling now.
Okay, I'll have fun. With you.
FUN!

BUDDHA'S CAKE

In the opened palm
Of Buddha's right hand
Is a round small cake,
Its message clear:
That life is sweet.

And we shall have a feast!
Some wine please
With the cake!

And now a magic cup appears,
And full to overflowing, reminding me
To see my life as not half full
And not half empty, but like the cups
In Dante's Heaven where everybody's cup's
A different size, and everybody's cup
Is full to overflowing,
So there's no comparing
Anybody else's cup with mine,
But only seeing all the fullness of my life
And celebrating how it's full --
With love and health and trees and birds,
My pen now also pouring words,
So that this poem, too,
Is full to overflowing.

MY SUITOR DISAPPOINTS

"Take it with a grain of salt,"
My Laughing Buddha counsels,
"This new suitor is a joker,
He says, 'There is no meaning to our lives,
We're all mistakes of nature.'
That's how he survives.

"I know you're disappointed, sad
Because you think he has to be like you --
Ecstatic, finding meaning, feeling;
But how can we not smile and think
That everyone is different?
So Vive la difference! It's silly, sweet.
Surrender, Janie, to its grace.

"Two years ago when you first
Put me in this garden
It was on barely growing grass,
And look around me now! You'll see
At least six different plants that live together,
All in harmony: the rosemary; the five o'clocks;
The clover; and some new green leaves
The name of which you do not even know,
With laughing, open faces,
And all of it green, green,
Green surrounding me where once

Was only dry, bare ground!

"Of course I'm laughing!
Think: those mystery leaves,
You don't know where they're from
And sure enough each leaf,
Splayed open like a snowflake, is
Doubtless different from the others --
Like you and this new suitor!
Oh what a glorious garden it is and
How can we not laugh,
And even with delight?!

"And also don't forget that
Just as you have pulled the weeds
Out of the ground around my base,
The rye and prickly marigolds,
The foxtails and the puncture vines with burrs,
Trust that soon you'll know
If you must weed this suitor from your life
Because he doesn't make you laugh
But makes you too, too sad."

HOW DARE I BE DEPRESSED

How dare I be depressed
Because I am "laid low"
From laryngitis or a cold
Or stomach problems, tummy-bloat,
Or feeling so alone?

I look outside: and there he is
Reminding me of all the joy that's in the world,
Laughing, deeply, endlessly,
True mirth in his belly,
His gut even distended (Like mine?
But surely not from crazy eating?)!
Perhaps he's heard a joke?
I WANT TO HEAR
THE PUNCH LINE!

I sit down next to him,
Cross-legged on the ground,
He feels like my friend.
How easily my hand rests on the top of
His bald, round, sturdy, happy head.
He comforts me, I comfort him.
I brush some leaves off his shoulders.

His left leg's folded
On the ground in front of him,

The sole of its foot is opened to the sky,
A foot that he could surely use for walking,
But no, he's happy just to sit there,
Laughing.

His other foot, its right knee bent,
Is planted on the ground
As if to show that he could walk or even sprint,
Except that there's that cake
That's waiting in his open hand.
Perhaps he's laughing at
The thought of running
And that pastry flying in the air!?

Or is he laughing at me
Perhaps too poised between my eating cakes
And bounding into the world,
Into confused careers, relationships,
Or fixing up my house,
As if my sitting here were not enough,
Sitting smiling here delighted
At the endless joy in the world
The endless beauty in the world,
The ecstasy unfolding.

PAINFUL INDECISION

I'm at a crossroads,
Don't know
What I want to do
With the rest of my life.
I tell my Buddha.

"Laugh," he says,
"That is your assignment.
Master that,
The answers
Will come."

WORRY

Please. Could I not take everything
So seriously, and be at least a bit like you,
My Laughing Buddha? You laugh at it all:
Sunshine, earthquakes. You laugh if it rains;
If it floods, you laugh, as if knowing that in spite of it
Or that because of it, that all will be well.

I mean to let go worrying,
I sense that all this worrying
Is just the same as saying prayers
For all the things that make me scared.

Let me focus instead
On your ample belly,
Think of all the perfect food
That you have loved and that you love,
Of how delicious it all is, has been,
And be a witness to your body's celebrating it
So visibly, rotundly: the tastiness, spiciness
The chicken dumplings, wines, the breads and sweet cakes
All sustenance for LIFE.
Let me focus on your ample belly,
Proof that you have had enough, and have enough;
And let me understand that I, too, have enough
And always will.

I see you there, so happy in my garden,
The wooden ducks I gave my mother
Bleached and weathered at your side,
Unlike your stolid stone, unweathered ballast,
Strong as the courage that I seek,
Courage unweathered and immutable.

I HAVE WRITTEN A BOOK

I have written a book about
My early childhood incest
And I'm scared to see it published
Fearing retribution or embarrassment,
People shunning me,
The topic "too heavy"
For too many.

My Buddha simply will not take this seriously!
"Are you kidding," he laughs,
"It's all part of this Perfect Cosmic Joke!
Think of it: because of what your Grampa did to you
When you were three years old,
Forty-one years later you scream and scream
At a virtual stranger who touches you
In an unconscious, stupid way
And all because your body, not your brain, is sure
The stranger is your Grampa?!
Think how random, mysterious
And outrageous your wiring must be
(Perhaps the wiring of the universe as well?)
How unfathomable the connections in your brain,
The synapses lighting up in pathways
With patterns you will never understand!
Why should you?! Just enjoy the light that sparks
Those neurotransmitters and their seemingly

Haphazard meetings and explosions,
And marvel at the light,
The shining, unexpected light.
The light.
Focus on the light."

DATING

"I have a blind date," I tell my laughing Buddha.
And he laughs. I say, "I'm nervous."
Buddha laughs again. I'm serious and ask,
"But what if he were Mr. Right?"
Buddha parries, playful, "What if he were Mr. Wrong?"
I smile and then confess that
"Either way, I guess I'm scared
The man won't like me."

Buddha, wise, responds
"Pretend he's me;
And that way you will know
That everything about you is
Just fine."

BUDDHA'S TREE

They say the Buddha
Was sitting underneath
A fig tree
When he found
Enlightenment.

I too have gained
Much knowledge
From the trees
That I have known;
And figs have kept me regular,

So maybe that is all we need
To keep us laughing:
The enlightenment of trees
And some figs.

GREEN STONE

The man who sold my Buddha to me
Told me he was made of
"Green stone,"

Though nowhere in the statue
Do I even find a fleck of green
(Things are seldom what they seem!).

The man explained the stone
Is "sedimentary, as formed
Through pressure, heat and time"
(Like me)
And that its specks are "harder rocks
Or fragments from volcanoes"
(Also like my own)

So where does Buddha end
And I begin?

LESSON

I bought a simple statue
Made of stone
I never knew
That it would be
My teacher.

Part III.   2014.   Endless Laughter

THE BODY LAUGHING

O Laughing Buddha,
That laugh!
Mouth open, lips curved upwards
Not unlike a crescent moon!
Or the shape of my eyelash
Floating down in front of me!

Or the bottom edges of my eyelids closed!
Or the curve of my earlobes,
Not as long as yours, dear Buddha, but mine, too,
Have smiling shapes holding them up
So they are falling down and laughing up.
Ha, ha, ha, ha, ha.

I look down at my breasts
And see the top halves of my nipples
Grinning up at me
Likes the wrinkles on the tops of my knees
When I straighten my legs.
My tummy's bottom line is smiling, too
(Only partly from the silly, perfect
Smokey-cheesed pizza I just ate).

The bottoms of the lobes of my lungs
Are laughing -- as they should be:
Without them you would never hear

My giggles and guffaws!
And even my belly button's
Curling upwards!
Ho, ho, ho, ho, ho.

How could I not have always known
My body was smiling and laughing
All the time?!

THE BONES OF THE BUDDHA

I hear it on TV:
That scientists confirm
"The actual bones of the Buddha!
Have been unearthed
In two thousand twelve!"

And still we know that everybody's DNA,
Descended from the stars,
(The same in stone or in our bones)
Is never changing,
Buddha living everywhere
Forever,

So I can only smile to think
That even in my statue made of stone,
The Buddha's bones
Are still alive
And laughing.

DISCOVERY

O sly Buddha Doctor,
You sit, icon,
Your medicine a mystery
For centuries,
And now, in Los Angeles,
The Medical Center
At UCLA
Has one entire Research Center
With scientific studies showing laughter
Causes our bodies to produce a chemical
That fortifies our immune systems!
Not only when we laugh,
But even
If we smile.

BUDDHA CAME FROM INDIA

Perhaps today my Buddha's laughing
Since he knows about a band of children
From Calcutta's slums
Who organized themselves and marched
Right into India's Parliament
To ask that laws be passed
So that the water where they live
Be drinkable, that laws be passed
So they and other kids could go to school!
Perhaps he's laughing since he knows
THE LAWS WERE PASSED!!!

I learned this from a documentary
And saw the girls and boys --
All in brightly colored clothing,
Orange jackets, turquoise skirts,
Purple pants and red and yellow shirts.

My Buddha's stone is only grey
But his laughter has more colors
Than all the colors of the rainbow, more music
Than infinite symphonies.
All laughter does.

THE DEER

Buddha's laughing! Yes, it's funny --
Me, I'm laughing too:
The deer had eaten all my roses,
Flowers, branches and the thorns!

For weeks and months they ate,
Despite the fake coyote pee, the garlic oil,
Despite the hair, then soap, then mothballs
Hung like Christmas ornaments
In little pouches on my bushes.

Then John, the man who keeps raccoons away
From fish in ponds, arrived and put
Some metal boxes on my roof;
He said that they could sense
The moving deer and then emit a sound
To scare the deer away.

And now, just six days later
My roses bloom again!
Take that you hungry, disrespectful deer,
Ravishing my bushes of their beauty,
You hyper-hungry deer,
You noble, beautiful, rose-famished deer!

HA HA HA THIS TIME WE GOT YOU!

I'VE GOT MY ROSES BACK!
HA HA HA HA!
GO EAT SOMEONE ELSE'S ROSES!
HA HA HA HA!

PHOTO OF ME AT THREE

There I am in the photo,
LAUGHING,
Maybe I'm three and a half.

Is my father there,
Behind the camera,
Making me laugh?

Or is it possible
That little girl
Can see and understand
The Laughing Buddha?

HAND CARVED

The jolly man
Who found my Buddha for me
Says he was "hand carved."

Whose hand, I wonder,
Worked how many days
Or weeks, or months,
To give me now
So many years
Of pleasure?

JOY, RETURNING

Oh, my Buddha,
After a long trip
I return to you!
I don't know what you have thought
Or witnessed or known
Since we were last together,
But whatever it may have been,
Here you are
Still laughing.
Such wisdom.

WRINKLES

Many women I know have facelifts
To tighten their cheeks
And eliminate the lines
Around their mouth and chin.

I have my share of lines as well
But pay someone to cut me?
Ha, ha, ha, ha, ha.

When all I need to do is smile
And all the wrinkles disappear!

THROUGH THE SEASONS

Through the seasons
He just sits there,
Is.

The frost kills the vines above him
They turn brown and fall on him.
Summer brings more green around him
And flowers, chamomile, rosemary, lavender
And through it all, he sits there,
Is.

Autumn, spring, the changing seasons,
Leaves fall
New shoots sprout
But Buddha, my Buddha
Just sits there,
Is.

DEATH

"Death?" says Guru Mai,
"I've met him.
He's a barrel of laughs."

Is he like you, then, Buddha --
Full of jokes, a ticket maybe
In his pocket to take us unimagined places
More miraculous than Paris,
More fun-filled than a Coney Island ride?

Maybe he's more fun
Than a barrel of monkeys,
Though who are those monkeys, anyway
And where are all those barrels from?
And how'd those monkeys
Get there in the first place?!

I guess we're all just barreling along
Towards Death's next unknown stopping place --
Might as well have a good ride,
Laughing all the way.

SMILING BUDDHAS

Now I learn that
In the Shanghai Museum
Are many smiling Buddhas,
Not laughing, mind you,
Just smiling.

It's like I skipped a grade!
Went right from
Crying to laughing.
Quick journey.

Good one.

LAUGHING DOG

My Buddha's been with me
For almost three years now,
He's watched me lose old neighbors,
Seen the new ones,
Seen me lose my old dog,
Seen the new one,
And the new dog laughs.

He laughs! Perhaps because he's called
A "Poodle" mix and knows
French poodles come from Germany;
Or laughs because his breed is famous for
Its curly, fuzzy fur and he arrived here shaved
Because of all the burrs and foxtails in his coat
From days of roaming, lost and starving,
His left front paw infected, on the streets.

He laughs! Perhaps because the dog
Knows how to walk on just his two hind legs
And jump and prance and run and pose
Like any well-trained circus dog --
BUT DOESN'T SEEM TO KNOW
TO PEE OUTSIDE?!

Perhaps he laughs because he knows
When I was ready for this second dog

I told our local Rescuer of Dogs
I didn't want my new one to be white
Because my old dog had been white,
And then I told her (since I couldn't help it)
"She was also luminescent,"
And he knows that when the woman rescued him,
She called to say that though the dog was white
He wasn't really "luminescent," but instead
"A different kind of white" —
(Would you have guessed
The woman's also selling Real Estate?) --
Not that I could tell exactly what
The new dog's color was because,
When he showed up, the dog was shaved!

The bottom line is now I have
A new and laughing dog,
Color of arborio rice or baking soda,
His nose and lips and eyes all black;
And though I know that
Nothing's either black or white
I know that I will keep this dog
And that he's happy here with me,
He's fed, he's safe, he's loved,
And, finally, he has a home.
Of course he's laughing!
Ha, ha, ha, ha, ha, ha, ha!

That laugh! It's joyful, playful --

Like my Buddha's,
The new dog's laughing mouth
Is open also like my Buddha's,
His teeth are showing, like my Buddha's.
HE'S LAUGHING LIKE MY BUDDHA!
HA HA HA HA HA HA HA!

And me, I'm laughing too,
I'm laughing more
Than I have ever laughed before.

Ah, the magic of
The Buddha
Laughing.

ACKNOWLEDGMENTS

My thanks go to Brian Gibson, who had the patience and perseverance to continue to search for Laughing Buddhas for me until I saw the one I wanted; to Jennifer Strom, who has had the generosity and grace to continue to remind me I am a poet; to Alex Dennett, for her calm, intuitive, and amazing support; to Bonnie Loren and Pamela Shaw, who read everything I write, and have for a very long time, who, just by reading my words, help me to believe they are worth reading; to Terry Belanger, who printed a rare and spectacular version of my first book of poems; and to Jill Bayor for always believing in me as a poet.

Thanks, too, to Rachel Chodorov, Linda Harris, Jan Barry and Eileen Peterson, all smart and all generous enough to have read this book, and others, giving me the courage to send them into the world; to Janet Kelly for her joyous and unwavering support that makes my books visible to people I don't even know; to Timothea Stewart for her spontaneous generosity; and to Dolly Gordon for her wisdom and special friendship.

My thanks also to Yogi Alan Finger -- there was never a class he taught in which he wasn't laughing; to the great Buddhist teacher, Thich Nat Than, for describing Buddhism simply by laughing for a very long time; to Rabbi Stanley Levy, for letting me laugh for four minutes in temple as Abraham's wife (the Bible describes her LAUGHING!); and to W.S. Merwin, for support the importance of which he will probably never know. Lastly, a huge thank you to my Uncle Larry Elow for his always intelligent and robust enthusiasm for my writing; and to Ahmed Aboudan, Ariel Fantasia, and Santina, Justin and Lee Oppmann, for their gifts of love and family -- which mercifully have the power and grace to get us all TO LAUGH.

JANE MARLA ROBBINS

A National Endowment of the Arts Poetry Grant finalist, Jane was commissioned by the Kennedy Center to write and perform the one-woman play, *Reminiscences of Mozart by His Sister*, which she also performed at Lincoln Center in New York. Her one-woman play in verse, *Miriam's Dance*, about Moses' sister, was produced in New York and Los Angeles. Also in New York she starred in her three-character play *Jane Avril* (translated into Danish, produced in Copenhagen). Her Obie-nominated one-woman play, *Dear Nobody*, which she co-authored with Terry Belanger, ran for a year Off-Broadway, was produced on CBS, and toured to London and all over the United States. Her one-acts include: *Bats in the Belfry* (Spoleto Festival); *Cornucopia* (winner, University of St. Thomas One-Act Play Competition); and *Norman and the Killer* (a co-adaptation for PBS). Her two-character play, *A Radical Friendship*, about Martin Luther King Jr. and Rabbi Abraham Heschel, with Ed Asner as Rabbi Heschel, was seen in Los Angeles in 2014. A New York production is planned for 2015. Jane is also author of the successful self-help book, *Acting Techniques for Everyday Life*, and its accompanying deck of cards, *Perform At Your Best*, which won the Gold Axiom Business Book Award. She teaches acting, poetry and playwriting, privately and at universities and corporations. A graduate of Bryn Mawr College, an essayist for the Los Angeles Times, author of the chapbook, *Dogs in Topanga*, Jane has acted on Broadway (*Richard III, Morning, Noon and Night*); in film (*Rocky I, Rocky II, Rocky V, Arachnophobia);* on TV *(ER, The Heidi Chronicles*); and with Circus Flora as the Ringmaster Clown. You can see her reading some of the poems in this book on YouTube. For more information please see janemarlarobbins.com.